He's a nice man,

she thought with a pang. He's kind and thoughtful. But I'm going home in two weeks and we'll never meet again—and I'm too old for a holiday romance. I probably always was! I was never the type to throw myself into a brief affair, even before I married Rob. I'm far too conservative

and cautious....

Dear Reader,

The Seven Deadly Sins are those sins that most of us
are in danger of committing every day: very ordinary
failings, very human weaknesses, which can
sometimes cause pain to both ourselves and others.
Over the ages they have been defined as: Anger,
Covetousness, Envy, Greed, Lust, Pride and Sloth.

In this book, I deal with the sin of Lust. We can all
become driven by desire, especially when we fall in
love; it is a natural human instinct, and can be
beautiful—but lust can also have an ugly face and
express the very opposite of love. Sometimes lust is
born of hatred and a desire to destroy.

Charlotte Lamb

This is the fifth story in Charlotte Lamb's gripping
seven-part series, SINS.

ALSO AVAILABLE IN HARLEQUIN PRESENTS
SINS

Charlotte Lamb

Dark Fever

Harlequin Books

TORONTO • NEW YORK • LONDON
AMSTERDAM • PARIS • SYDNEY • HAMBURG
STOCKHOLM • ATHENS • TOKYO • MILAN
MADRID • WARSAW • BUDAPEST • AUCKLAND

ISBN 0-373-11840-6

DARK FEVER

First North American Publication 1996.

CHAPTER ONE

BIANCA FRASER woke up on a cold, raw February morning and remembered with a sinking heart that it was her fortieth birthday. Outside, it was raining; inside, it was cold, because the central heating hadn't yet automatically switched itself on; it was set to come on at seven; and it was dark because it was only half-past six and the sun hadn't yet risen.

She didn't have to get up yet; her alarm was set for seven-thirty because this was just another working day. She had to shower and dress, get breakfast, drive Tom to school and Vicky to work and then get to work herself by nine. The day stretched out bleakly in front of her, heavy with responsibilities and chores, and she did not feel like getting up.

Turning over in the warmth of the bed, she found herself reaching out towards the accustomed hollow in the centre, but it was empty, as it had been now for over three years.

Closing her eyes on a wave of misery, she pressed her hand down into the mattress where Rob's body had lain beside her for twenty years. They had gone so fast, those years; it only seemed like yesterday that they had met, fallen in love, married. Time flashed past her closed eyes, under her lids, images vanishing into oblivion.

'Oh, Rob,' she groaned, remembering the feel of his body close beside her all night.

She missed him most of all when she was in this bed, alone. Her body ached for his; she quivered and groaned at the memory of his touch, his passionate mouth, his body coming down on her. It was so real; she put her arms out to hold him and felt his warm, naked skin under her hands.

'Oh, Rob!' she whispered in pleasure as he moved against her. Running her fingers through his hair, she looked up at him with passion, needing what he was doing so badly that it was almost unbearable.

But it wasn't Rob. A strange face looked down at her; it was a stranger's body on top of her.

A scream choked in her throat and she began to fight him off, writhing and kicking until she rolled right off the bed.

As her body hit the floor her eyes flew open. The room was no longer dark; grey morning light filled it. Trembling in shock, Bianca struggled up and looked dazedly at the bed.

It was empty.

Breathing thickly, her heart beating so fast it deafened her, she looked hurriedly around the bedroom. That was empty, too. There was nobody here but her. A second later, her alarm clock began to ring, the noise shockingly loud in the silence.

That was when it dawned on her. She had gone back to sleep; she had been dreaming.

Scarlet, then white, she jumped up, staggering a little, turned off her alarm and rushed to the bathroom. In the room next to hers she heard Vicky's alarm endlessly jangling until there was a loud moan, the sound of someone heavily turning in bed and the alarm stopped dead.

Bianca used the lavatory, turned on the shower, stripped off her nightdress, all without thinking what she was doing. Her mind was on automatic pilot. She

was in shock. The dream was still playing in her head;
she was remembering her passionate response as some
total stranger did that to her...

Shame made her skin burn. How could she have felt
like that? Responded to a stranger? It if had been
Rob...but it hadn't been! I thought it was! she de-
fended herself hurriedly. At first I thought it was, until
I saw his face.

But dreams don't come out of nowhere; you dreamt
what you wanted to dream.

No, that's not true! she thought angrily. She could
not accept that. She hadn't wanted to dream about some
strange man making love to her; she had never even
thought of such a thing, not in her waking moments.

My unconscious...she thought, biting her lip. But she
knew it wasn't that simple; she couldn't dismiss it as
something conjured up without her knowing anything
about it. It had been her who was dreaming about a
stranger making love to her.

And who was he, anyway, that stranger who had
shown up so mysteriously in her dream? Who had she
substituted for Rob?

She tried to remember something about him—anything—but his face was blank, she couldn't recall a thing
about him, except that it had not been Rob. There had
been no sense of recognition, or familiarity—she must
have conjured him up out of her imagination, an admission that made her blush.

Oh, for heaven's sake! Dreams didn't mean a thing,
anyway! When you were asleep your mind ran haywire,
conjuring up a cinema show made up of memories, imagination, fantasy.

She looked at herself in the mirror, a woman of forty,
with long, loose black hair hanging down her back,

widely set apart blue eyes with pale lids, fine black brow
her face really still quite smooth considering she was no
officially middle-aged. No wrinkles anyway—unles yo
counted a few laughter-lines around the eyes and mouth
a faint sadness in the eyes, too, because grief carved i
impact on the face as much as laughter did.

She pulled a face at herself angrily. At your age yo
should have stopped fantasising. That's for kids. You'r
not a kid any more. Forty today! I can't believe it. Wher
did the time go? Is that a grey hair? She peered at
closer, decided it was just the way the light fell, but
would come soon, of course. Age was a juggernau
rolling down on you; you couldn't get out of its wa
Before she knew it she would find herself with grey hai
lined skin...how long before she had false teeth? O
shut up! she told herself and turned to step under th
shower, pushing away the depression creeping up on he

Mornings were closely timed in this house; there wa
a lot to do before they could all start their day and sh
needed to concentrate.

When she was dressed, had put on light make-up an
combed her hair up into a smooth chignon at the bac
of her head, she knocked on Tom's door and got a sleep
groan from him.

'Get up, Tom! It's a quarter to eight!' He had an alar
clock, which would have gone off by now, but it neve
seemed to wake him up. Fifteen and healthily active fror
morning till night, when he did go to bed and sto
running and jumping around, Tom could sleep on
washing-line and would probably sleep through a
earthquake. She had to bang on his door every mornin
before he woke up.

Vicky came out of her room without prompting
yawning, brushing her short, curly fair hair. Althoug

her mother found it very hard to believe, Vicky was now nineteen, and for two years had been working in a large department store which insisted on its staff wearing what amounted to a uniform—a black skirt, white shirt and black cardigan. Staff could buy them in the store at a generous discount, and could wear any style they chose, so long as they kept the overall colour scheme. Black and white suited most women; on Vicky they looked exceptionally good because of her blonde colouring. She wore her clothes with panache, moving gracefully on high black heels. Her skin had a warm pink glow, her eyes were large and bright and her pink mouth a cupid's bow. Vicky was pretty and was enjoying her life so far, although she had recently begun to put on a bored expression and talk with what she believed to be sophisticated cynicism.

'God, what horrible weather. Raining again,' she said, and her mother smiled to herself at the drawling tone.

'Yes, it's going to be another wet day.'

Downstairs, Vicky put on the kettle for tea or instant coffee while Bianca made porridge for breakfast; Vicky looked at it with horror. 'No, thanks—all those calories!' She poured herself orange juice, had her usual tiny slice of thin toast. She was barely five feet two and was terrified of putting on weight, which, admittedly, she did easily.

Tom rushed in, having apparently dragged on his school uniform anyhow before splashing cold water on his pink face but not bothering to put a comb through his straight dark hair.

Bianca was pouring his tea. She looked at him and made a face. 'Oh, Tom! You look as if you've slept in your clothes!'

He grinned, a large envelope in one hand, a brightly gift-wrapped parcel in the other. 'Happy Birthday, Mum!' He bent over the table to kiss her on the top of her head.

'Oh, thank you, darling,' she said, smiling up at him. She had begun to wonder if they had forgotten—usually their father had reminded them.

Vicky looked guilty. 'Yes, Happy Birthday, Mum. I'm getting your present later today; I'll give it to you tonight.'

Over her head Tom mouthed something at his sister; Bianca suspected it was rude from the glare Vicky gave him. They argued all the time; sometimes she wondered if they always had, or if it was only since their father died; she didn't remember them being so ratty with each other when Rob was there—or was it simply that they had changed since they began growing up?

Grief gnawed inside her again. Rob would have loved to be there to watch Tom play for his school, score the goal that won a match...

She looked at the birthday card blankly for a second, then made herself look properly. It was funny—a cartoon with a joke message; she laughed and handed it to Vicky to read.

'Oh, ha ha,' Vicky said disagreeably, dropping it on the table.

'Don't you get porridge on my card!' Tom said, snatching it up again.

Bianca unwrapped the parcel, which turned out to hold a tiny bottle of French perfume; she unstoppered it with some difficulty and almost reeled from the musky scent. She always wore light floral perfumes, and could not imagine herself wearing this, but she smiled at her son who was watching her eagerly.

'Mmm...gorgeous... Thank you, Tom. I love it.'

'Put some on, then!' he urged.

She cautiously dabbed a little behind each ear and Tom leaned over to inhale the smell.

'Great,' he said in satisfaction.

Bianca caught Vicky's eye and silently warned her not to make one of her tart comments. Looking at the clock on the kitchen wall, she said, 'Time's getting on... Sit down Tom, and eat your porridge. We'll have to go soon.'

He threw himself into his chair and picked up his spoon. 'This is a porridge sort of morning, isn't it? Listen to that rain. Are we going out to dinner tonight, for your birthday? We always used to when...'

He stopped and looked at her and Bianca swallowed, a bitter pang of sadness hitting her.

'Yes, Dad always took us out on my birthday—I think that's a great idea,' she said gently.

She had told them to talk about Rob whenever they felt like it, she wanted to keep him alive for them, but these spiky little moments were always happening; they would start a sentence then remember, and look at her guiltily. Were they over their grief but aware that she wasn't? Bianca felt that sadness again, shadowed by a sense of guilt towards her children—it was quite normal, after all, for people to get over a death; she didn't blame them for that. After Rob died she had determined to be both mother and father to them—she hadn't wanted to make them feel they must never mention their father in case they hurt her. She wanted to set them free to enjoy their lives—not make them anxious and uncertain.

'Let's eat Chinese!' Vicky suggested.

'Oh, yeah! Terrific,' said Tom.

'OK, I'd like that,' Bianca said, picking up her cup and draining the last of her coffee. 'I'm going to get the car out of the garage—hurry up, you two! Don't forget your briefcase, Tom—and your games kit.'

The rain fell in the same relentless way as Bianca drove to work later, having dropped off her children. It was still raining later when she was dressing the window of Zodiac Fashions, the little boutique she and a friend ran.

'We did much better with the January sales than I'd dared hope, and I'm really pleased with the new spring styles. I... Are you listening? What's the matter with you?' Judy Turner suddenly realised that Bianca had stopped work and was just standing in the window, gloomily gazing out into the almost empty, rain-washed street.

One hand absently tucking stray strands into the otherwise immaculate chignon in which she habitually wore her black hair, Bianca turned round, sighing. 'Apart from this weather, the fact that I am now forty, and that I'm utterly fed up, you mean?'

Judy put down the account books she had been working on behind the counter. 'I'll make the coffee, you watch the shop, then you can tell me all about it.'

'I just did!' Bianca called after her departing back, then got on with the window-dressing, easing a bright yellow dress on to a haughty-looking model whose arm kept getting stuck in one position.

Bianca normally enjoyed this job; it gave her a chance to indulge her creative streak, finding accessories to go with a garment or a season, making the window look so attractive that women hurrying by simply had to stop to look at it. Today she wanted an air of spring; she had put a line of little yellow fluffy chicks along the front, sprays of pink apple blossom were pinned on the sides and the models would be carrying spring flowers—all artificial, of course, but they were surprisingly real-looking and had cost far more than real flowers would have done. You could use them again and again, however, which made them cost-efficient.

When Judy came back with the mid-morning coffee, the window was almost finished, and she went outside briefly to assess it, coming back with a smile. 'It looks great! I love the chicks—pity we haven't got a mother hen to go with them. You've got a real flair for window-dressing—didn't you say you once went to art school?'

'I started at college, taking an arts course, but then I met Rob and by the end of my second year——' Bianca broke off, a little pink, laughed, and finished, 'Well, I was pregnant, so I left without finishing the course.'

Judy laughed too. 'The old, old story. But couldn't you have gone on with your studies? Why did you have to leave college? Were your parents difficult?'

'They weren't too pleased at first, but they were very good about it. That wasn't why I left college. I can't blame anyone else for that. It was my decision. I simply wasn't interested any more. I had this strong urge pushing me along—I wanted my baby, I wanted to be a wife and mother; I didn't want college. Later on I wished I hadn't been so stupid and I could have kicked myself for not finishing my course, but at the time all I knew was that I was obsessed with going along a different road.'

'Did Rob feel the same?'

'He was very keen to get married, too. He was much older than me and he wanted to start a family, have a home. So we got married in a hurry, my parents gave us some furniture, his parents gave us the deposit on a flat. Rob had a good job, of course, so we could manage without me going out to work. I stayed at home and looked after Vicky. I didn't want to leave her with some stranger. I wanted to look after her myself.'

Bianca's dark blue eyes were smilingly wistful as she sat down to drink her coffee. 'I sometimes think those were the best years, those first years, we were so happy!'

'You still miss him, don't you?'

'Every day.'

Judy gave her a look in which affection and concern mixed with faint impatience. 'It has been three years, Bianca! You should be over it by now. I mean... I know you loved him and the two of you were very happy together, but you can't go on grieving forever; it isn't right. Life has to go on, and, after all, you're still young.'

'Forty isn't young!'

'Oh, for heaven's sake, forty isn't old either—you're in your prime! No wonder you're fed up. I bet you haven't had sex since he died.'

Suddenly scarlet as she remembered the vivid dream she had had a few hours ago, Bianca almost spilled her coffee.

'Honestly, the things you say!' she spluttered.

'It isn't just men who need sex, you know,' snorted Judy. 'Women have the same urges. We're just not encouraged to face up to it. Have you even been out on a date yet?'

'Mind your own business.'

'Has anybody asked you out?'

'Judy, stop it! What's got into you?'

'You give off stop signs,' Judy told her bluntly. 'Any man who looks at you gets that old "don't even think about it" signal, so they back off fast. Men need encouragement. They need to be sure they won't get their faces slapped if they so much as ask you out.'

'I'm not looking for another man!' Bianca told her fiercely. 'I'm too old to start again with someone else. Anyway, I've got the children to think about.'

'They aren't going to be around all the rest of your life, Bianca. They'll grow up and move out, get flats, get married—it's only natural; they'll soon be adults who need their own lives.'

'Not for years yet. Tom is only fifteen!'

'And when he's twenty you'll still only be forty-five. I bet Vicky gets married young. She's so pretty, she's going to be swamped with men. When they're both gone, what will you do? You could live to be eighty—all on your own!'

A shiver ran down Bianca's back.

Judy saw the change in her face and said coaxingly, 'Do something about yourself—change your hairstyle, stop wearing those boring pale pink lipsticks, get some sexy clothes.' She leaned over to sniff. 'I like that scent, by the way—that's more like it—something musky and mysterious, not that wishy-washy lavender or rosewater you've been using for years! You could have men dropping from the trees if you took some trouble.'

Bianca thought of that as she walked down the busy street to lunch at a small bistro later, leaving Judy to take care of the shop. As she passed under a bare-branched poplar tree amusement lit her blue eyes at the idea of men floating down from it to land at her feet, like a Magritte painting.

By one of those strange coincidences life threw at you, a second later she looked into a travel agent's window and there was the same image again.

The window was dominated by a large poster advertising holidays in Spain; out of a bright blue sky floated men in bowler hats and dark suits, carrying umbrellas, coming down to land on a golden beach, a blue sea foaming up on the sand, with girls in revealing swimsuits sunbathing under striped umbrellas, and in the background were white hotels, black bulls, glasses of red white, a pair of flamenco dancers, the man all in black, with a tricorn hat, the girl in a bright red flared dress, her black high heels tapping out the rhythm of the dance.

It was so colourful and vivid, full of sunshine. Shivering in the cruel wind, Bianca pulled her warm coat closer and longed for the sun.

Maybe Judy was right. Perhaps it was time she did something about herself. Oh, she wasn't looking for a man—but she must do something about the way she felt, shake herself out of this grey depression.

Was that what her dream had meant? She went red again and hurried into the travel agent's.

That evening she didn't get home until half-past six; she was tired and cold. As she parked her car she remembered that she had agreed to go out to dinner at the Chinese restaurant a couple of streets away, and was grateful that she wouldn't have to cook dinner tonight as she did most other nights.

She stepped out of her wet boots and left them to drain in the porch. She was so sick of this endless winter. She had to get some sunshine soon or she would go crazy. She hung up her dark pink woollen coat before putting her head round the door of the lounge.

Her two children were watching a video and didn't even look up. Bianca considered them wryly for a second. There was no family resemblance between them; a stranger would never guess they were brother and sister. Fifteen-year-old Tom, sprawled on a sofa, as relaxed as if he were boneless, his long, slim body limp, had changed out of his school uniform and was now wearing the inevitable jeans and a blue sweater, his hair the same colour as her own, his eyes the same widely spaced dark blue, and Vicky was sitting in an armchair carefully painting her nails a strange dark plum. She was far more like her father than her mother, with corn-coloured hair and hazel eyes, except that she had a petite, pocket Venus figure instead of Rob's height.

'Hello, Mum, have you had a good day? Isn't it cold outside? You must be frozen; come and sit down by the fire and I'll make you a lovely cup of coffee,' Bianca said loudly.

Her son, Tom, did look round then, grinning as he tossed his untidy hair out of his eyes. 'The little men in white coats will come for you if you keep talking to yourself.'

'I have to. Nobody else around here will. Are you both ready to go out for this Chinese meal?'

'Yes, Mum,' Tom said, his attention riveted on the screen again. 'Do you really want some coffee?'

'Not if we're going out at once. Are you ready, Vicky?'

Vicky stirred, blew on her fingers. 'I'm ready, but I can't go yet—it would ruin my nails and I only just painted them.' She looked round, waving a plum-tipped hand at a small table on which lay a red-foil-wrapped box. 'Oh, that's your present there, Mum. Happy Birthday.'

Bianca unwrapped a box of Chanel make-up, her eyes widening. 'Why, thank you, Vicky, that's wonderful.' She hoped Vicky hadn't spent too much on the expensive cosmetics; it had been very generous of her.

'I know you don't usually wear those colours, but I think you should—you need an image change!' Vicky said. 'My friend Gaynor is on the Chanel counter; she

picked out the colour scheme for you; she said they'
suit you.'

Bianca fingered them all in their matching packaging
a glossy dark red lipstick, eyeshadow boxes in a trio o
shades, from light blue to brown, a cream foundation
and loose powder in a compact.

'I can't wait to try them.' Somebody else trying to d
an image change on her! she thought crossly. First Judy
now her own daughter... What was so wrong with th
way she looked?

She opened her shopping bag and took out a holida
brochure, her blue eyes brightening. 'How do you tw
feel about a winter holiday? Two weeks in Spain..
sunshine, beach life, flamenco dancing?'

'Great—when?' asked Tom without looking round.

'As soon as we can fix it!'

'What...now?' He looked round then, aghast. 'You'r
joking, Mum. I've got matches fixed every Saturday fo
weeks. I can't go away. We'd lose if I wasn't there.'

'Big head,' Vicky told him.

'It's true,' he insisted indignantly. 'I'm their bes
striker! Ask anyone. I get all the goals. I can't go awa
during the season—they'd kill me.'

Vicky said casually, 'I can't go either, Mum. Actually
Drew and I were thinking of going to Majorca some tim
in the spring——'

'Drew can come with us!' Bianca interrupted.

Vicky's look revealed first blank incredulity, the
scornful amusement. 'Drew and me...go away with you
Come off it, Mum! You don't think I want my *mothe*
around, do you? Anyway, we were thinking of going o
one of these under-thirty holidays. No old people ca
go on them.'

'Old people?' repeated Bianca, outraged.

Vicky gave her a quick, half-laughing look. 'Well, you're not old, of course; I didn't mean you, I meant . . . Well, you know what I meant.'

Oh, yes, she knew what Vicky had meant. Her daughter did not want her around when she went on holiday; she was the wrong age group. Her son was too absorbed in his own life to want to go away at all. Her spirits sank. She had been looking forward to getting away to the sun, but she couldn't go alone; she hadn't had a holiday alone for . . . She stopped, frowning, realising with a shock of surprise that she had never had a holiday alone. Before she met Rob she had gone away with her parents, and then she had always gone with Rob and the children. She had never once gone anywhere alone.

Well, it's time I did, she thought. Judy was right—she had to start adjusting to the idea that Tom and Vicky were growing up, would one day leave home. She had to build a life which did not revolve around them.

'I'll go away alone, then,' she said, and they both turned to stare at her, mouths wide open in disbelief.

'Alone?' Vicky repeated.

'You mean you're going to leave us on our own here?' Tom's eyes sparkled. 'For two whole weeks?'

She could read his mind; he was looking forward to two weeks without supervision, without anyone nagging him to do his homework, do his daily chores. Tom hated doing housework, but Bianca insisted that he helped out, did as much as his sister. She had been determined not to bring up a useless boy who expected women to do everything for him. She had a brother like that. Jon had never had to lift a hand at home; their mother had waited on him hand and foot, and after Jon had married he'd expected his wife to do the same. Sara had resented it;

the marriage had broken up after a few years, with Jo
complaining that Sara was unreasonable, and Sara bit
terly accusing him of being selfish. Jon had marrie
again, but his second marriage was far from contented
it seemed to be drifting on to the rocks exactly the wa
the first one had.

Bianca didn't want her son turning out like Jon. Sh
had shared out work equally between her two childre
In the kitchen was a computer-printed rota pinned u
on the wall; Vicky and Tom each had jobs to do ever
day.

Bianca expected them to keep their own bedrooms tidy
and inspected them once a month to make sure they wer
actually doing the work, but they also had to help he
keep the rest of the house tidy, do the shopping, hel
prepare meals for them all. Bianca, too, had a rota, whic
was pinned up next to theirs, so that they should kno
that she did twice as much as the two of them pu
together. Which was more or less what they expected
of course, but it put a stop to claims that she was askin
them to do too much.

'And while I'm away there are to be no wild parties
or hordes of your friends wrecking the house!' she tol
Tom, who looked at her innocently, blue eyes wide as
child's.

'No, Mum.'

'I'll keep an eye on him,' Vicky said with suspiciou
sweetness.

'It applies to you too, Vicky. I'll hold you both re
sponsible for anything that happens, remember.'

She had been encouraging them both to be respon
sible ever since their father died. Before she made an
decision she had carefully asked their opinions, an
listened to them seriously.

After Rob's death she had had the choice of living, with difficulty, on a small fixed income for the rest of her life—or taking the risk of investing some of the money from Rob's insurance in a business which might give them all a comfortable income.

After talking it over with Vicky and Tom, she had decided on the latter course. Judy, who was a close friend and long-time neighbour, had enthusiastically offered to put up fifty per cent of the money and share the work in running the business. She had recently inherited money from her father, and wanted to put it to work in a more interesting way than simply investing it in stocks and shares. Her husband, Roy, was a travelling salesman who was away a good deal, her children were grown-up, and Judy was tired of working in other people's shops; she'd wanted to run her own.

Bianca had explained to Tom and Vicky that she could only manage to work six days a week if they were prepared to help in the house, and they had both agreed. They had more or less kept their bargain, too, even if reluctantly at times.

'Are we going to the Chinese or not?' she asked them both crossly now. 'Or shall I make some beans on toast?'

They gave each other a silent but eloquent look, then smiled soothingly at her, getting up.

'We're ready, Mum!'

Now they were going to be indulgent, as if she were a half-wit. A pathetic *old* half-wit. Resentment churned inside Bianca as she drove them to the restaurant. Some birthday she had had! It had begun with depression in bed that morning and it was ending in much the same mood. And now I'm forty, she thought. Forty! She had a terrible feeling that from now on life was going downhill all the way.

* * *

A week later she landed at Málaga airport in very different weather. She came out of the airport building in
a world of blue skies, sunlight and palm trees, and stood
there for a moment feeling her winter-chilled skin quiver
in disbelief. Then she hurried off to collect the hire car
she had booked in advance before setting out on the
motorway to Marbella. The drive took longer than she
had expected, largely because of heavy traffic, but
eventually she found the hotel.

Bianca would not be staying in the hotel itself; she
had booked an apartment in the grounds, which were
extensive, with large white adobe-style buildings scattered among trees and lawns intersected by winding
narrow streams running under arched wooden bridges
in something like the Chinese style. Each building con-
tained half a dozen separate apartments, each with its
own front door and a balcony looking over blue
swimming-pools and gardens down to the sunlit blue sea.

The apartments were spacious; Bianca found she had
a bedroom, bathroom and sitting-room, one corner of
which was a tiny kitchen area, with everything you might
need to prepare a meal.

She unpacked rapidly, explored her new domain,
showered and put on a stylish green linen dress and white
sandals. The hotel served a buffet lunch at one o'clock
and it was just after twelve now. She would take a walk
through the grounds before going to lunch. As she was
on holiday she wouldn't want to spend her time
cooking—she was going to eat out a good deal.

She went out on to her balcony and leaned on the rail,
staring down over a pool right below the building.

There was someone swimming in it. Through the blue
glare of the light on the water Bianca saw a shape

moving, a black seal's head, a powerful, gold-skinned body cutting through the pool.

Shading her eyes, she watched as the swimmer slowed to a standstill, at the edge of the pool, before hauling himself out of the water. He stood on the blue and white tiles for a moment, raised his hands to slick back his dripping black hair. She stared at the wide, smoothly tanned shoulders, the deep, muscular chest, the slim waist and strong hips, the powerful thighs and long legs. His wet black swimming-trunks clung to him, almost transparent in the strong sunlight, so that he might as well have been naked.

She couldn't look away. Her mouth went dry and her skin prickled with heat.

At that instant, as if some primitive instinct warned him that he was being watched, the stranger lifted his head to stare in her direction.

Her face burning, Bianca guiltily turned and almost ran back into her apartment.

CHAPTER TWO

BIANCA went into Marbella itself that evening, in th
hotel courtesy coach, to tour the local tapas bars wit
a guide. The other guests in the party were all marrie
couples, which made Bianca feel left out and kept re
minding her of Rob, and what wonderful holidays the
had once had. Even before they arrived at the first ba
in the old town she was beginning to wish she hadn
come, because nobody much spoke to her. It wasn't unt
they moved on to another bar that she got into conver
sation with another of the party—a woman of about he
own age with short blonde hair and blue eyes.

She was sitting on a bar stool beside Bianca studyir
the contents of a tapas saucer. 'Is this what I think
is?' she asked Bianca, who peered at it too.

'Squid?'

The bartender was watching them—he suddenly leane
over and grinned. '*Calamares a la plancha*!' he e:
plained, then went off to serve someone else.

'You speak Spanish?' the German woman aske
Bianca, who shook her head.

'But I think *plancha* means plate.'

They called out to their Spanish hotel guide for
translation.

'Squid cooked on a hotplate!' he called over. 'Dor
be scared. Try some! You don't have to fight the bul
to be brave, you know!'

Bianca and the other woman laughed, tried the squ
and had to agree it was good, if a little rubbery.

24

'Too much garlic in it for me, though.' The German turned to smile at Bianca. 'We ought to introduce ourselves—I'm Friederike Schwartz; please call me Freddie—everyone does.'

'I'm Bianca Fraser.'

Freddie stared and laughed. 'Bianca...that means white, doesn't it? And Schwartz means black in German. How funny.'

'Your English is amazing! I'm terribly impressed. I barely know six words of German.'

'My husband works for a big German company—we travel the world with him, my children and I. He once spent two years in America, so we all learnt English.'

'Is he here with you?' Bianca glanced around the crowded little bar trying to guess which of the men belonged to Friederike.

'He is the guy with a red tie, playing dominoes at that table,' Freddie told her. Bianca inspected him, smiling.

'He's very attractive! Lucky you!' He was clearly older than his wife, a man approaching fifty, bronzed and slim, brown-haired, brown-eyed, with a touch of silver at the temples, and still very good-looking.

'Yes, I am, but he is cross tonight. He didn't want to come on this bar cruise. Karl does not like to be out late. He wanted to stay in our suite looking after our children, but I talked him into coming.'

'How old are your children?'

'Teenagers. I keep telling him they don't need baby-sitters any more. We have two sons, twins aged fourteen, Franz and Wolfgang, and my daughter Renata, who is seventeen and getting prettier all the time. When I walked around with her men used to stare at me—now they stare at her! I feel like the wicked queen in Snow White. I look into my mirror and grind my teeth every day.'

Bianca did not take her too seriously—she was laughing as she said it and was much too lovely to feel threatened even by a daughter who was half her age. Freddie was probably in her early forties but she looked ten years younger—her skin was smooth and unlined and her eyes were bright and clear. Her figure was slim and her clothes classy.

Karl looked up and saw them watching him and beckoned to his wife. Freddie groaned. 'He's going to ask when we can go back to the hotel! He's bored already.' She slid down from her bar stool and smiled at Bianca. 'Nice talking to you. See you later.'

Bianca sipped her glass of red wine doubtfully—it tasted like red ink. She couldn't help feeling that she sympathised with Freddie's husband—she wasn't enjoying this evening much either. But it would have been depressing to stay in her apartment by herself.

'You are alone, *señora*?' asked the Spanish guide, sliding into the seat beside her.

She gave him a wary look, nodding, hoping he was not going to make some sort of pass. A short, dark-skinned man in his thirties with a distinct paunch, he was not her type. But all he said was, 'Then please be careful not to leave the group. Keep with us at all times. I am afraid handbags have been snatched lately. There are some gangs in town, from other big towns—they work in pairs, going around on motorbikes, and they're so quick—they come up behind you and snatch your bag, and they've gone before you know what is happening.'

'I'll be careful,' Bianca assured him, taking a piece of chorizo, the spicy red local sausage, from a little tapas saucer.

'Enjoy, *señora*,' he smiled, getting up to go and talk to some of the other guests.

They moved on a few minutes later to another bar, another selection of tapas—the other guests grazed eagerly on the food on offer while they drank their glasses of wine, discussing the various dishes with each other. Bianca noticed that Freddie and her husband had disappeared; perhaps they had taken a taxi back to the hotel.

The range of tapas was bewildering—artichokes in vinaigrette, baby clams served in a garlic sauce, fried whitebait, baby eels or squid, snails, mushrooms in a rich tomato sauce, chorizo, hard-boiled eggs stuffed with a variety of things. Everything was beautifully cooked but very rich.

The last bar they visited was the best—along with the tapas there was music and flamenco dancing, a black-jacketed man urgently drumming the heels of his highly polished shoes, his partner dancing with passion and invitation around him, her red skirts flaring.

The sexual tension in the music and dancing did something drastic to Bianca's mood. She was flushed and feverish as she clapped along with the others and drummed her feet, as they were instructed—the rhythm of the music had got into her blood.

When the dancing ended the bar seemed even noisier; as the evening went on and more and more people piled inside until there was hardly room to move. Bianca began to get a faint headache. She needed some fresh air so she wriggled through the crowded bar and went outside into the cool Spanish night.

She had no intention of going far; she would just wait in the street for her companions to come and join her. They would be leaving soon, she imagined—it was getting very late.

The cool air was delicious on her overheated skin; she stood there breathing in for a minute, sighing with pleasure, feeling her headache easing off, and then, across the narrow street, she saw a small boutique and was struck by a dress displayed in the window. It reminded Bianca of the dress the flamenco dancer had worn—low-necked, tight-waisted, full in the skirt, and a vivid red. She walked over to take a closer look. It was stunning on the window dummy—she wasn't sure she had the nerve to wear it in public, it was so dramatic and eye-catching; her children were bound to laugh at her. But she was tempted. She had the right colouring and she was slim enough to wear a dress like that.

She frowned, trying to work out the price in English money, and was vaguely aware of a motorbike roaring round the corner from the main square and heading towards her.

It slowed as it reached her, someone jumped off it, and she saw another reflection move in the glass window of the boutique beside her own reflection. A small, slim figure in black leather, the face hidden by a black helmet, was running up behind her. The motorbike had skidded to a stop a few yards on along the street.

With a start, Bianca remembered the guide's warning about motorbike thieves. Her nerves jumping, she swung round, just as the black-clad figure grabbed for her handbag. She instinctively opened her mouth wide and began to yell, holding on to her bag like grim death. The fact that she couldn't see the face of her attacker made the whole thing more frightening.

After trying to yank her bag away the boy let go and pushed his hand into his black leather jacket—the hand came out holding something. In the street-light's yellow gleam she saw steel glittering and her throat closed in shock. He was holding a knife.

Everything seemed to go into slow motion. She stared at the long, razor-edged blade, frozen, saw the black-gloved hand holding it, the black leather cuff of the boy's jacket not quite meeting the glove.

Between them there was a red line etched in the tanned flesh—a knife-cut, she thought dumbly, and somehow the sight of the scar made the knife real. She went into panic, backing away, so scared that she had even stopped screaming. The knife slashed downwards. For a second she thought he was stabbing her—then she realised what he intended. He was trying to cut the straps of her handbag.

Her fear subsided a little, but, because she had been really scared, now she got angry. She had once been to a short self-defence class at the local evening school; she remembered what she had been taught, and brought her knee up into his groin, hard.

He gave a gasp of pain and staggered backwards, then recovered and came at her again with the knife, muttering in Spanish. She didn't know what he said—his voice was muffled by his helmet—but it sounded very unpleasant, and she knew that this time he was not trying to cut her handbag straps—he wanted to hurt her. The air throbbed with hatred.

A second later a car came round the corner. The yellow beam of its headlights lit them as if they were on a stage. She turned to face it, waving urgently, shouting, 'Help! Help!'

The black-clad figure on the motorbike shouted out in Spanish and turned the bike to come back towards them. Snarling, the other boy climbed on to the pillion, made a very rude gesture at Bianca with his black-gloved hand, then they rode off at high speed and disappeared.

Bianca sagged against the wall, her knees turning to jelly, trembling violently now that the adrenalin had gone and reaction had set in.

The car screeched to a stop and a man got out and strode towards her, saying something in Spanish. She weakly lifted her head and the light of the street-lamp fell on her face and showed her his—they recognised each other in that instant. He was the man she had seen swimming that morning.

'Are you OK? Did he hurt you?' he asked in a deep, husky voice, his grey eyes moving over her in search of some visible sign of injury.

She shook her head, feeling even more like fainting. Why did it have to be him who came along just at this moment? It seemed less like a coincidence than a punishment. He was the last man she wanted to see right now.

'He wanted my handbag,' she whispered.

'Did he get it?' His English was very good, but she heard the faint note of a foreign accent. Presumably he was Spanish. He was certainly very dark, with olive skin and black hair which was glossy and very thick.

He was very casually dressed, in cream linen trousers and a chocolate-brown shirt, worn without a tie, the collar open at the throat to give her a glimpse of the bronzed skin she had stared at that morning when he'd climbed out of the pool. The very memory of that moment sent a wave of heat through her whole body. From a distance she had found him devastating—at such close proximity he had an even deeper impact on her.

'No,' she said unsteadily, showing him her handbag which she still clutched in one hand. Then she broke out in a voice that shook, 'He had a knife!'

She still couldn't believe it. It would be a long time before she got over the shock of seeing the knife shining in the lamplight. Nothing like that had ever happened to her before; she had always led a rather quiet, peaceful existence; violence was something she had only read about in newspapers. She had never imagined it happening to her.

'I saw it. As I was driving towards you I saw the knife he held and I thought he was trying to kill you—you're sure you aren't hurt?'

She was wearing a little black jacket over a white dress printed with lilacs. He reached out to touch her shoulders and arms lightly, his fingertips gliding over the material of the jacket in exploration.

She quivered helplessly, shaken to her depths by what she instantly felt—his fingertips left a trail of fire on her skin through the layers of material under them.

'No, I...I'm not... He didn't hurt me...' she stammered.

'You're cold,' he said, his frown even deeper. 'That's shock. Come and sit in my car. I'll call the police.'

She urgently said, 'No, please don't—I don't want to spend hours talking to policemen; he didn't get anything, or hurt me, so... I couldn't even describe him; he was wearing a helmet that made it impossible to see his face; he looked like a spaceman.'

His face tightened in disapproval. 'You ought to tell the police about it—he's dangerous; he might use that knife on someone else and they might not be as lucky as you were.'

She knew he was absolutely right; it was what she would have said herself to anyone who had been attacked like that. How different a situation looked when it was you, yourself, who was experiencing it. Her common sense and reason told her one thing, she felt another.

Sighing, she said, 'Well...could you ask if I could talk to them tomorrow? I really don't feel up to it tonight.'

He stared down at her, his face still hard. 'Very well, I'll get in touch, explain what happened; I shall have to give evidence too, because I witnessed the attack. I'll ask if you can talk to them tomorrow. Come along, I'll drive you back to the hotel.'

She resisted the hand that tried to lead her away. 'I'm with a group from the hotel—they're in that bar; they'll come out looking for me any minute.'

He shrugged her refusal away coolly. 'I'll go in and speak to the guide—it's Ramón tonight, isn't it?'

Startled, she nodded. 'Yes.' How had he known that? Had he been on this tour himself? Or did he work at the hotel?

He had such a marvellous tan—he must surely live here to have got so brown at this time of year. That tan was not the product of a week or two in Spain. It spoke of months of exposure to the sun.

'Sit in my car and I'll have a word with him, then I'll drive you back.'

Bianca was so shaken by what had happened that she didn't argue, although in other circumstances she might have done. She was too independent and used to running her own life and taking care of herself and her children to enjoy being ordered around by some strange man. But tonight she was quite relieved to be able to let him take charge; she let him lead her to his car and slide her into the front passenger seat.

He left the door open, but instead of going straight into the bar he went round to the back of his car and was back a moment later with a warm woollen tartan car rug which he gently wrapped around her.

'It gets quite cold at night at this time of year,' he said as she looked up, startled, her blue eyes wide, the pupils dilated as she felt his hands moving over her. 'And you're probably still in shock. Just sit here and rest. It will only take me a minute to find Ramón and explain.'

He closed the car door and she watched him walk rapidly over to the bar; the light from it spilled out around him as he opened the door and went in, his black hair gleaming and his face in sharp profile, his nose long and straight, his mouth a ruthless slash, his jawline determined.

Not a man you would want to argue with, and few people probably ever dared—which accounted for his cool assumption that she would obey him.

That could get annoying! she thought wryly, her mouth twisting. If she weren't feeling so weak at the knees just now she would probably have resented being ordered around like that.

Or did she start feeling weak-kneed the minute she saw him get out of this car?

The idea made her tense and hurriedly shut her eyes as if that would make it easy to forget what she had just thought. It didn't, of course. She couldn't ignore the truth. Closer, and fully dressed, he was even more devastating than he had seemed at a distance, almost naked. She couldn't understand why he was having such an intense effect on her. When he'd wrapped this rug around her his hands had touched her and she had felt her body throb with sensations she was afraid to remember. Her face ran with hot colour, her mouth went dry.

With a pang she thought of Rob, and felt an instant stab of guilt. It was shameful to be feeling this way about some other man, a stranger she had only seen for the first time today. What's the matter with you? she asked herself. You have been on your own now for three years and you've met plenty of men during that time, some of them pretty good-looking—what's so different about this one? You're acting like a teenager with a first crush.

I wish I *were* a teenager! she thought. Well, maybe not a teenager—but I wish I were twenty again. I don't want to be forty.

Was that what it was all about? Was she desperately looking for some way to stop time? To go back to her youth?

She pulled the rug closer, glad of the warmth. She was still shivering, her skin icy and her body weak with shock.

Her birthday had been a watershed, she realised. It had made her think about the way time was passing—seemed, in fact, to be accelerating. She hadn't noticed the fact until her birthday. She had been too busy looking after her children, learning to run the shop, coping with grief and loneliness. When she had thought about time it was only to remember lost happiness—it had always seemed as if only yesterday she had been twenty years old and falling in love with Rob, walking on air, looking forward to marrying him, starting a family, believing blissfully that they had an eternity together in front of them. She gave a long sigh which wrenched her body. That was the best time of my life. I wish I could have it back again, she thought.

But you could never have time back. It flowed, like a river, in one direction, on and on without stopping, and you could never swim back upstream. You had to go on with the river.

She heard a sound and opened her eyes again to see the door of the bar opening. He was coming back.

He walked quickly, long-legged, easy-moving, the night wind making his black hair blow back from his forehead, making his shirt ripple against him in a way that made the planes of his upper body very visible.

She stared at the wide, muscled shoulders, the ribs and flat stomach of a man in the peak of condition, swallowing, aware of her pulses going crazy. She had never met a man who had this effect on her; it was really beginning to spook her.

He opened the door and got back into the car and she was immediately tense, wildly conscious of his closeness, of the proximity of their bodies in that small, enclosed space, of the faint scent of his aftershave, his long legs stretching out beside her own. Sensual pleasure went through her in waves, making her mouth dry, her skin hot, her ears beating with hypertension.

'I found Ramón and explained,' he said, starting the car and glancing at her at the same time. 'He was horrified when I told him what had happened. He wanted to come out to make sure you were OK, but I told him I'd look after you.' The car began to move slowly as he added drily, 'He also tells me he had given the usual warning about never leaving the party and going off on your own.'

Flushing, she admitted it. 'Yes, he did, but...'

'But you didn't think it could happen to you?' His tone was sardonic and she felt her skin prickle with resentment. He obviously thought she was stupid, a silly woman with no common sense.

'It was very hot and crowded in the bar and I needed some fresh air; I didn't think it would be dangerous just to step outside; I didn't mean to go anywhere else. But I noticed a dress in a shop window so I went over to look at it and——'

She broke off, swallowing as she remembered the moment of panic as she'd faced the knife. She had been stupid; she couldn't deny it. His cool censure was justified. She had no excuse for her folly. She had been warned, and had taken the warning lightly. 'It happened so fast, there was no warning,' she whispered.

'There never is; they don't give their victims a warning, they're ruthless and vicious,' he said drily. 'You were lucky it didn't end in tragedy—he might have used that knife and you could be on your way to hospital now, or a slab in the morgue.'

She shivered and stared out of the window. He was right. She had had a narrow escape. What would have happened to her children if she had been killed tonight?

As he drove through one of the squares, she stared at a large stone fountain, the spray of water shooting out of a nymph's hands, glittering in the lamplight, rainbow coloured. A group of young people in jeans and T-shirts ran out of a narrow, winding street and danced across the square, laughing and singing under the bare-branched, pollarded lime trees.

The car drove on along another road, between white houses, their window-boxes filled with little pink flowers, their shutters closed over the windows behind which, no doubt, people were eating—in Spain they ate dinner very late, often at nine or ten o'clock at night.

A few moments later he drove out of town and headed down the motorway which ran along the Costa del Sol from Málaga to the border, with golf courses and new villa estates on their left, the sea on their right, a distant gleam of silvery water under the moon.

She sighed. 'It's so lovely here, it's hard to believe anything violent could happen.'

'Well, it could,' he said impatiently. 'Just remember—it could happen anywhere, any time. We live in a violent world—whether we live in London, New York, Spain or anywhere else—it's wise to be careful, wherever we are.' He shot her another look. 'You're here for two weeks, aren't you?'

Her blue eyes widened. 'Yes—how did you know that?'

'I run the hotel, Mrs Fraser. It's my job to know who is in each apartment. We pride ourselves on our security—some very rich and famous people stay with us and they expect us to keep a close eye on who comes and goes in the hotel. I'm sure you've noticed our security men patrolling the grounds?'

Still absorbing the fact that he was the hotel manager, she blankly shook her head, her black hair flicking against her shoulder. He gave her another of his dry smiles.

'Well, they're here, day and night. Look out of your window some time and you're bound to see one. They wear uniform, they're armed and they keep in touch with base on walkie-talkies. Any disturbance is dealt with immediately; you need have no fear while you're in the hotel grounds.'

She was taken aback by this new revelation and shivered. 'I find that pretty scary—having armed men all around me day and night!'

He turned his head again, to look down into her blue eyes, his expression changing. His stare seemed to dive down into her very soul, and her heart made a frightening leap, like a salmon trying to fight back upstream against a powerful tide.

She hurriedly turned away, afraid that he could read her thoughts, her feelings—the very last thing she wanted him to do. She had to hide her reactions from him; he must not guess how he was making her feel. None of this was real; it wouldn't last; it was some sort of hormonal thing, she decided. Neither her heart nor her mind was involved—this was just her body acting up, a chemical reaction which would pass if she ignored it.

'Your first name is Bianca, isn't it?' he said softly. 'A lovely name—it suits you; you look like Snow White with your black hair and blue eyes and that lovely skin. Bianca is an Italian name, isn't it? Have you got any Italian blood?'

She shook her head, keeping her eyes on the busy traffic through which they drove.

'My name is Marquez,' he said. 'Gil Marquez. The rest of my name is far too long to remember. I won't bother you with it; just call me Gil. I was the last child and first son my mother had—before I was born she had three girls. She was forty when I was born. The doctor said she shouldn't have any more children, so my father gave me all his favourite names—six of them!'

'Six first names?' she repeated, startled.

He grinned at her. 'He was an extremist—I'm afraid I take after him. He named me after three of his favourite saints, and added the names of his two brothers—Gil was his father's name, so that came first, and that is the one I use.'

'He sounds wonderful,' she said, wondering what he meant by saying that he was an extremist, like his father. He certainly had the bone-structure of one—fierce, sharp, insistent planes, piercing eyes, a strong mouth and an arrogant jawline. She could imagine him in armour, in medieval times, fighting with ruthless implacability. He was an all-or-nothing man, not someone comfortable and easygoing.

Nothing like Rob, she thought, and guilt stabbed inside her again. Why did she keep comparing him with Rob?

They were chalk and cheese, physically and mentally, such totally different men that it was ridiculous to compare them. Ridiculous, and shameful. Rob was her own dear love; she would never love like that again. She never wanted to! What she was feeling about Gil Marquez was a spring madness, infatuation, crazy, unreal. She wished to heaven she had never stood on her balcony and seen him climb out of the water, his body glittering gold in the sunlight.

Maybe the sunlight and the foreign nature of this place had something to do with her inexplicable reactions to Gil Marquez, these turbulent feelings? She was away from everything familiar, everything safe. She was alone, for the first time in years, without her family—a woman without responsibilities, without boundaries, out of touch with reality for a while, free. Had that freedom gone to her head?

'He was,' Gil said, and she looked at him again blankly, at first not realising what he was talking about. Then she remembered that he had been talking about his father, and the past tense registered.

'He's dead?' she said with sympathy.

He nodded, his face unsmiling now, his eyes fixed on the road ahead and a frown carving itself into his forehead. 'A year ago. He was eighty-five, he had had a good life, but it was a shock to all of us.'

'Death always is,' she said with sympathy, watching
his sculptured profile, and he turned to give her a
searching glance.

'I noticed on your registration card that you were a
widow. How long has your husband been dead?'

'Three years.'

'Three?' A pause, then he asked, 'How long were you
married to him?'

'Twenty years.' A lifetime, she thought—the time she
was with Rob felt like her whole life; she found it hard
to remember the time before they married.

'And you were happy together.' It wasn't a question,
it was a statement, flat and unaccented.

'Yes.'

Another pause, then he said, 'You haven't re
married—haven't you met anyone else, or——?'

She stiffened, resenting the curiosity, and interrupted
sharply, 'I have two children and a business to run. My
life is quite busy enough.'

His grey eyes flickered mockingly over her. 'What a
waste!'

She felt hot colour sting her face. 'I don't like dis
cussing my private life with a complete stranger, Señor
Marquez!'

'How very English,' he murmured, his mouth flicking
up at the edges.

'I am,' she insisted. 'Very English.'

'Is that a warning?'

She shrugged and didn't answer.

'I'll bear it in mind,' he said drily.

They were approaching the hotel complex, she was
very relieved to see. He was forced to give all his at
tention to slowing down in order to make the right-hand
turn into the grounds. They were very pretty at night

coloured fairy-lights in the trees facing the road, glowing globes of lamps standing on all the paths between the trees and beside the apartment blocks.

As they drew up outside the hotel they heard music from inside. The hotel was also brilliantly lit; through the plate-glass windows they saw a crowd of people in the piano bar, drinking at tables or dancing on the polished wood floor, or standing around the white piano listening to the man playing it.

Gil Marquez turned to face her, one arm draped over the steering-wheel, his lean body gracefully lounging against the seat, one knee brushing hers, making her even more aware of him.

'It takes a while for shock to wear off, Mrs Fraser; our resident nurse should take a look at you before you go off to bed.'

'I'm fine,' she said, sliding out of the car.

It was unfortunate that her foot skidded under her on the damp surface of the stone path—an automatic water spray was whirling among the flowerbeds near by, and some of the drops of water had fallen on the path, making it very slippery; she had to grab for the car to stay upright.

She heard Gil mutter in deep, angry Spanish, then he was out of the car and beside her, his arm going round her waist, his fingers just below her breast; she felt her body quiver in primitive arousal.

Drowning in sensation she thought, He mustn't notice; he mustn't realise what's happening to me. Her knees had gone again; she could barely stand up, she was trembling so much, and she had to yield to his support, her body leaning on him.

He bent to look at her. 'Are you going to faint? Don't argue again—you're going to see our nurse, whatever you say. Can you walk?'

'Of course I can!' she protested. She pushed his hand down and moved away from him to take the steps up to the hotel. They were marble and as slippery as the path; she had to move carefully.

Gil watched her for a few seconds, then said something in fierce Spanish under his breath. She didn't know what he had said, but it made her nerves jump; his voice sounded like the crack of a whip.

He came up behind her, his arm going round her waist again, lifting her off her feet, apparently without effort. His other arm went under her legs and she found herself being carried against his chest; her head swam, and she let it fall against his arm, shutting her eyes, afraid to look at him for fear of what he might read in her face. She heard the curious buzz of voices in the hotel foyer, though, and felt her face burning. People would be staring. What on earth would they be thinking?

Someone spoke to Gil in Spanish and he answered without pausing in his stride across the foyer. A moment later she heard a door slide shut and then she knew they were in a lift which was rising smoothly.

Where was he taking her?

The lift stopped, he walked out, and Bianca lifted her lids enough to see that they were in a hotel corridor, deeply carpeted, calm, silent. He wasn't taking her to his room, was he? Alarm bells rang inside her.

She opened her eyes fully and said huskily, 'Please put me down, Señor Marquez. I'm OK now—I want to go to my own apartment, please.'

He had paused in front of a door. He looked at her, his mouth twisting. 'No need to get agitated, Mrs Fraser.

This is only the surgery. I haven't brought you up to my room to make a pass at you.'

She went bright pink. 'I didn't think you had!'

'Oh, yes, you did; that's why you're having palpitations and trembling like a leaf!' he drawled.

Bianca wished the floor would open up and swallow her. Instead, the door opened and she hurriedly looked at the woman standing there—a small, thin, dark woman in a nurse's uniform with a neat white cap. Behind her Bianca saw a sparcely furnished room with white walls, venetian blinds on the windows, the usual paraphernalia of a doctor's surgery—a desk, chairs, a tall screen on wheels, a high trolley with leather padding for a patient to lie down on.

The nurse smiled politely, spoke in Spanish to Gil and he answered in English, so that Bianca could understand him, which she thought was very thoughtful of him.

'This is Mrs Fraser, Nurse Santos—she is staying in one of our apartment blocks. She was attacked in the street by a mugger—she doesn't seem to be hurt, but I think she is in shock. Will you look after her while I go and ring the police?'

'Sí, of course, señor.' Nurse Santos took Bianca's arm firmly. 'Please . . . come in, Mrs Fraser. How you feel?'

Gil vanished, closing the door behind him. Nurse Santos sat Bianca down on a chair and asked her a few questions, examined her, took her pulse and temperature, her blood-pressure, then smiled.

'OK, no problem, Mrs Fraser.' She had a much stronger Spanish accent than Gil Marquez. 'Heartbeat a bit fast, not serious. You need sleep, to be quiet, quite OK in morning.'

There was a tap on the door and the nurse called out in Spanish. The door opened and Gil glanced in, raising his brows. Nurse Santos said something else in Spanish and he nodded. 'Well, that's good.' He looked at Bianca. 'Nurse Santos doesn't think you're going to die just yet.'

'I know, she told me,' she said, very aware of him and trying to hide it. She turned to smile at the nurse. 'Thank you for taking care of me.'

'Not at all, my pleasure.'

Bianca stood up. 'Well, I'll follow your instructions and go back to my apartment and get some sleep. Goodnight, Nurse Santos.'

She walked out of the door and Gil came after her. 'I'm afraid you can't just yet.'

She stopped and faced him, frowning. 'What do you mean?'

'The police have asked to talk to you tonight—don't worry, they're coming here to interview you. I told them you were in a state of shock and they won't talk to you for long, but you must see them tonight. They have a pair of suspects picked up after another attempted mugging. This time they knocked the man out; he's still unconscious so your evidence could be very helpful to them at this stage. You can talk to them in my office. It's on this floor, at the far end of the corridor. Not far to walk!'

She couldn't refuse. Reluctantly she followed him to a door which bore a brass plate with the word 'MANAGER' on it. Gil ushered her inside and followed, closing the door.

She paused to look around, taking in the large, leather-topped mahogany desk, with its bank of telephones, a pile of papers on a leather-framed blotter, a silver-framed photograph and behind the desk a leather swivel chair.

'This is where you work?'

He nodded. 'Would you like something to drink while we wait for the police?' He gestured to a modern cream-covered couch on one side of the room. 'We'll be more comfortable over there.'

She didn't like the sound of that, but he took her elbow and steered her to it.

'Would you like a brandy? It might calm you down.'

'No, thank you. I'd much rather have some orange juice—if you have any.'

He nodded and opened a cabinet on the wall, which held a mini bar; he got out glasses and poured her chilled orange juice, poured himself some whisky and added a dash of soda. 'Ice?' he asked over his shoulder.

'No, thank you; it waters the juice down.'

He carried the glasses over and sat down beside her, handing her the juice.

She sipped, anxiously watching out of the corner of her eye as he swallowed a mouthful of whisky. He was sitting far too close; his knee was touching hers. She could hear the clock ticking on the wall, hear the intake of her own fast breathing.

She felt his eyes wandering over her and her alarmed glance shot to him and away again. She tried to think of something to say but her mind had frozen; her body was entirely in control of her.

Any minute he was going to touch her. She knew it. She wanted it, which was worse. But she was terrified.

When someone knocked on the door she almost jumped out of her skin. Her orange juice shot over the rim of her glass and fell on her skirt. She frantically rubbed at it, trembling.

'My God, your nerves are shot to hell, aren't they?' Gil Marquez said, staring, then he called out something in Spanish and the door opened.

Two Spanish policemen stood there. Gil got up and put down his glass, went over to shake hands with them, speaking to them in deep, grave Spanish. Bianca struggled to pull herself together, grateful for the fact that he stood between her and the policemen.

By the time she had to face them she was more or less in control of herself again and was able to answer their questions calmly enough.

They did not stay long. Clearly, her replies were disappointing to them; they had hoped she could give them a good description of the faces of the two men, but she had never seen their faces, and could only guess at their height and weight, and describe the bike they had been riding.

After asking her to go down to the police station next morning to attend an identity parade, they left, and she immediately told Gil that she wanted to go back to her apartment.

He didn't argue this time; he walked her to the lift and took her down to the ground floor. As they went out of the exit into the garden they walked past the blonde German woman Bianca had met in the bar that evening. Freddie didn't notice Bianca, but she did do a double-take as she spotted Gil Marquez.

'Gil! There you are! We had just given you up. What happened to you? You were supposed to be having a drink with us. Did you forget?'

'I'm sorry, Freddie,' he said, kissing her lightly on both cheeks several times, French style. 'Something urgent delayed me.'

'Fine sort of brother-in-law you are!' Freddie teased him. 'Well, come on, let's go into the bar now and have a nightcap, then I'm off to bed.'

Bianca kept on walking, feeling faintly sick. Brother-in-law, Freddie had said. He was her brother-in-law. He couldn't be Karl's brother—Karl was German, and his surname was Schwartz. Gil was Spanish and his surname was Marquez. That could only mean he was married to either Freddie's or Karl's sister.

He was married, that was the important fact. He was not free.

'Bianca, wait!' he called from behind her, but she didn't look back, she merely walked faster, almost running.

A couple of minutes later she was safely in her apartment and locked the door, leaning on it in the darkness, groaning.

He was a married man. She put her hands over her darkly flushed face, humiliated and ashamed. If I'd known...

Well, thank God he doesn't know how I have felt ever since I first set eyes on him. And I'll make sure he never does know, either...

CHAPTER THREE

BIANCA found it hard to sleep that night; her mind was obsessed with images, contradictory and disturbing, filled with fear. However hard she tried she couldn't banish memories of Gil Marquez climbing up from the pool outside her apartment, his golden skin dripping with water, his black hair slicked back on his seal-like head. She turned over and tried to think of something else; her mind simply conjured up another, darker memory— the dark street, the sound of the motorbike, the black-clad figure, the steel flash of the knife...

She sat up and switched on the light, sipped some water, rubbed her scalp vigorously with both hands as if trying to erase the memory of those moments, then clicked off the light again and lay down.

At once Gil's face filled her mind—the hard jawline, the powerful features, the direct, assured grey eyes.

'Oh, go away!' she said aloud angrily, and she finally fell asleep in the early hours.

If she had dreams she didn't remember them when she woke up next morning. Through the closed shutters sunlight carved bars of gold across her room and she heard the splashing of someone in the pool outside, children's voices, the high morning calling of birds among the trees. She lay in bed staring at the wall, at the shifting shadows of branches cast there by the golden light, and felt as weary as if she hadn't slept at all.

Turning her head, she looked at the clock and was horrified to see that it was nearly ten. She hadn't got up

48

this late for so long that she couldn't even remember the last time. There was always too much to do at home—six days a week she had to get up to open the shop, and on Sundays she had to get up early to clean the house from top to bottom and do her personal washing. Her life was too crowded for her to have time for the luxury of sleeping late.

She could hear the hotel maids cleaning in the apartments above her: the drone of their vacuum cleaner, their voices, the slam of doors as they went in and out. They would want to clean her apartment next; she had to get up.

She groaned and slid out of bed, went into the bathroom. She felt better when she had showered; she put on her swimsuit and over that a short yellow cotton tunic. She decided to skip breakfast and have a coffee down on the beach; there was a bar down there which served a continental breakfast of croissant, orange juice and coffee. Bare-legged and wearing white sandals, she walked down through the hotel grounds, under tropical palms and exotic trees, to the beach, and found it half-full already.

Under striped blue and white umbrellas the matching loungers were laid out in rows. The young boy who was looking after the beach showed her to a place right at the front, near the sea, and put up an umbrella for her, adjusting the position to give her the right amount of shade over her mattress. Bianca asked him to bring her breakfast, tipped him, took off her tunic, folded it neatly, spread her towel over the striped cover of the mattress and sat down on top of it to smooth suntan lotion into her skin while she waited.

He was quick and efficient—he was back very quickly with a tray which he placed on the small plastic table

beside her. She paid him and he went off whistling whil
she drank her juice and then ate her croissant and dran
her black coffee, which was strong and very hot.

When she had finished she felt more alive. Lying down
she closed her eyes and let the sun permeate her pal
English skin.

'Good morning.'

The voice made her stiffen. She reluctantly openee
her eyes and saw him standing over her, his bod
blocking out the sun.

Her pulses went crazy at the sight of him in those brie
black swimming-trunks; the sunlight glinting on thos
smooth, tanned shoulders gave his skin a wonderfu
glow. Her eyes slid from them to the powerful muscle
chest, lean hips, strong thighs and those long, long leg
with their dusting of fine black hair.

She swallowed and managed a reply. 'Good morning.

'How are you this morning? Got over last night'
shock?' He coolly sat down on the empty mattress besid
her, only a foot away, and she was overwhelmed b
physical sensations that appalled her. They were on
beach full of other people, but she felt as if they wer
alone.

'Yes, thank you.' She was suffering another kind o
shock now; she had the feeling that it would be a lon
time before she got over this one. She wished, urgently
that she hadn't come down to the beach this morning
that she were somewhere else, anywhere but here. Wha
if he picked up on the turmoil inside her? The very ide
of it made her burn with angry self-disgust.

'You still look nervous, though,' he said, studying he
with narrowed grey eyes.

'I'm fine,' she muttered.

He looked unconvinced. 'You haven't forgotten that you have an appointment at half-past eleven?'

Bianca stared at him blankly. 'What?'

His brows rose. 'You obviously have! The police asked you to go down and identify their suspects at noon.'

Agitated, she looked at her watch—it was a quarter to eleven. 'How long will it take me to get to the police station?'

'Oh, only ten minutes, but if traffic is heavy it could take longer. We ought to leave by a quarter to twelve to be on the safe side, so you have plenty of time for a swim first.'

'We?'

He looked into her blue eyes, smiling crookedly, and her stomach sank as though she were in a lift which had suddenly dropped down at tremendous speed.

'I'll drive you there.'

'There's no need to... I can take a taxi.'

Coolly he said, 'I promised the police I'd take you myself, to interpret. You don't speak Spanish, do you?'

She had to admit that she only knew a few polite phrases. Her stomach tightened; it would be a nerve-racking experience, visiting a Spanish police station to identify the man who attacked her last night. She would rather never see the man again. But if she had to go she would be grateful for a little moral support and some help with the language. Only—why did it have to be him?

'I'm—I'm sure you're very busy, running the hotel,' she stammered. 'Couldn't one of your staff take me?'

'No, I said I'd do it and I will,' he said coolly, watching her in a way that made her even more nervous. What was he thinking?

She picked up her bottle of suntan lotion and began smoothing it into her sun-warmed legs again, to steady

herself, give her something to do which also provided
good excuse for not looking at him.

'Well, thank you; it's very kind of you to take so muc
trouble,' she said stiltedly.

Behind their barrier of lowered black lashes her blu
eyes were humiliated and angry. Once again she wishe
to God she had never gone out on the balcony yesterda
while he was swimming in the pool, had never seen hi
climb out of the water, golden and beautiful, had neve
felt that incredible, helpless surge of attraction.

She still found it hard to believe that this was hap
pening to her. She had loved Rob before she understoo
sensuality. Her first love had been innocent, as virgina
as untrodden snow; at eighteen she had been dewy-eye
and romantic, full of dreams, quite unaware of the po
tential that her body held. But she wasn't an un
awakened eighteen-year-old any more. She was a woma
who had learnt to enjoy physical passion, whose bod
clamoured for satisfaction it had not had for three years
Since Rob's death she had been so full of grief that sh
had forgotten she had a body, had put her sensuality t
sleep, in a sense. Now it had woken up and Bianca wa
alarmed by her body's increasing insistence.

There's a word for the way I feel but I don't like it
she thought. Lust—that's what this is . . . lust for a ma
I only met yesterday and who is married anyway—it'
disgusting. I must be out of my head. I can't believe thi
is happening to me.

'You hurried off last night without a word,' h
drawled. 'I was going to walk you to your apartment
but you had gone before I could catch up with you.'

She looked up and found him staring at her, his gaz
fixed on the rise of her breasts out of the tight cups o

ιe swimsuit, the soft pale flesh glistening now with oil
΄here she had applied the suntan lotion.

She looked away, her flush deepening, then said angrily
΄ith a pointed intonation, 'I thought you were going to
ave a drink with your sister-in-law.'

There was a little silence, then he said softly, 'Freddie
ιld me she had met you. She liked you. If you hadn't
urried off like that you could have had a drink with
s.'

'I was very tired,' Bianca said, hoping she sounded
onvincing. 'I liked her too—she's very friendly, isn't
he?' She took a breath, then asked deliberately. 'Is she
our wife's sister?'

He showed no sign of embarrassment or reluctance to
ιiscuss his wife. 'Yes, Mady is Freddie's younger sister.'

'Are they alike?' She was making herself talk about
ιis wife in the hope of reasoning herself out of this stupid
εeling for him. He was a married man, unavailable—
he had to stop this permanent drag of attraction
omehow and facing the fact that he was married should
ιo it.

'They're both blondes and built more or less the same,
ut they aren't alike in character—Freddie is a darling
nd Mady is...' He stopped and shrugged, his mouth
ιwisting cynically. 'Mady was the baby of the family,
εry spoilt; both her parents doted on her and gave her
ιhatever she wanted. Freddie was the eldest, though,
nd grew up with a strong sense of duty and responsi-
ιility. Nobody could accuse Mady of that!'

Startled, she stared at him. It didn't sound as if he
ιked his wife much—or was she reading too much into
ιis words? That would be wishful thinking; she must
ιop doing it. 'Do you have children?' she forced herself
o ask him, expecting an affirmative.

'None, thank God.'

Even more taken aback by that response, she stare frowned, and asked, 'Do you both live here at the hotel

There was a silence, then he said drily, 'Freddie did: tell you? I imagined she would have—Mady and I we divorced within a year of getting married. She left n and eloped with the man she's now married to—the live in Germany; he's older than her father but he worth millions and Mady is even more spoilt now tha she was as a child.'

A pulse began beating in the side of her throat; sl hoped he couldn't see it but he was watching her s closely that she was afraid he could. Increasingly she fe as if she was made of glass, and he could see everythir that was going on inside her.

He put out his hand suddenly and took the bottle suntan lotion from her. She tried to hold on to it but was slippery with oil, and slid easily from her grasp.

'Turn over,' he ordered.

'What?' She was still so absorbed in the realisatic that he was not married any more that she was too be mused to understand what he meant.

'Lie down and I'll do your back for you,' he said dril 'You can't do it for yourself, can you? And the sun hot; you don't want to ruin your holiday by gettir sunburn—it could be painful, especially as you have su lovely English skin, like strawberries and cream, all pin and white.'

She blushed at the compliment and laughed, but pre tested. 'I've got to go and change, to go to the polic station.'

'There's plenty of time yet. You particularly need protect the back of your neck and your shoulders fror the sun; you can get sunstroke just walking about here-

ou don't even need to be sunbathing. Lie down on your
tomach.'

He slid off the mattress he was sitting on and knelt
y her side. She looked up into his eyes and the world
ilted—sky and sea and yellow sands whirling. Dizzy,
he obeyed him and lay down, closing her eyes, falling
nto soft, velvety darkness, the world's wild spinning
gradually slowing.

All her other senses began operating with amazing
clarity, frightening intensity. Her ears were as sensitive
is those of a bat in a cave, picking up the singing of the
waves, the laughter of children, the cry of gulls overhead,
out, even more sharply, hearing the sound of his quick
oreathing, the trickle of lotion into his palm as he tipped
he bottle upside-down on his hand, the rustle of his hair
igainst his face as he bent over her. She almost felt that
she could hear the sound of his heart beating, the blood
circulating through his body.

She felt her breathing catch as he pushed her dark
hair up from her nape. Cool fingertips touched the
delicate pale skin left exposed. Her pulses leapt. He slid
his fingers down her neck, along her shoulder-blades;
she shuddered with pleasure. He pushed down the thin
straps of her demure, one-piece black swimsuit and
smoothed lotion where they had lain. His touch was both
soothing and hypnotic; she felt her pulses slowing, and
around them the sounds of the beach seemed to fade
nto the distance. Eyes shut, she drifted into a state where
he rhythmic movement of his hands dominated her.

And then she felt her tight-fitting swimsuit being pulled
downwards. She woke up in a hurry and tried to stop
he top peeling off, but too late—her breasts were already
oared. Giving a cry of dismay, she put her hands over
hem, angrily glaring at him over her shoulder.

'What do you think you're doing?'

'I haven't done some parts of your back which a half covered, and I don't want to get lotion on yo swimsuit.'

'That's quite enough!'

'There's no sense in half doing a job.'

He began working lotion into her spine, into the so cushions of flesh on either side of the indentation, h splayed hands kneading and moulding. She was ten for a moment and he felt it, murmured softly, 'Relax

She ignored him, but what he was doing was so i sidiously enjoyable that gradually she slackened, bega to drift back into a sensuous trance. Pleasure broke rainbows in her head—glittering and radiant, dazzli her. It was so long since a man had touched her in mately. She had slept cold and alone all this time, ar the sensual contact was both exciting and disturbing. Sl was trembling in response, hardly able to breathe, deep conscious of every lightest touch. He was kneeling ve close to her, his sandy naked legs brushing hers, his hanc strong and possessive, his body moving in a drivir rhythm which was a reflection of the act of love an made her blood run faster, desire ache, hot and dee inside her.

Her eyes shut tight, she was helpless, lost. If they ha been alone in a room instead of being here, on a crowde beach, he could have turned her over and taken her the and she knew she would have surrendered without struggle.

I want him! she thought, and that in itself was sha tering, because her husband had been the only man i her life until now, the only man she had ever slept wit the only man she had ever loved.

She didn't know how to deal with these new feelings. This deep clamouring in her body was entirely new to her. She had never before looked at a man and thought, I want him! She had loved Rob, had slept with him every night of their married lives and enjoyed sex with him—but this was very different.

She had been so young when she'd married Rob, and by the time she'd reached her sexual peak their love-making had been more of a ritual than an earth-shattering experience. Their love had become quiet and gentle; there had been no room in it for the sort of wild tremors shaking her now. It disturbed her to admit it, even to herself, but the truth was that Rob had never been a fiercely passionate man. He would have been shocked if she had shown him this side of herself.

I didn't know it existed! she thought, still stunned by these discoveries about herself. I never knew I could feel this way. Forty years old and I never knew myself.

Gil moved his hands in a smooth, rippling motion and her mouth went dry with desire. Oh, God! she thought, eyes closed, swallowing. I want to feel his hands moving like that all over me. I wanted to——

She stopped the thought, appalled. What is happening to me? I must be going crazy. Maybe it's because of the years alone since Rob died. Maybe the need for love has built up inside me day by day, without me re-alising it. She felt it then; it was all there under the surface, this terrible need, a feeling so hot that she was burning, so deep that it was as if she had been stabbed and was bleeding to death.

There they were, on a public beach, surrounded by other people—she could hear their voices, their feet scattering sand as they ran—people sunbathing, reading, sleeping, playing beach games, swimming, and she felt naked, exposed; she felt that anyone who looked at her must see what was going on inside her.

Her face was dark red, her heart beating twice as fast as was safe; she was terrified.

Don't panic, don't panic! she hurriedly reassured herself. Nobody will have looked twice. People on a beach take very little interest in each other.

To convince herself of that, she opened her eyes and focused on the people in her line of vision, and noticed that some of the women were topless—and there were lots of people rubbing suntan oil into themselves—their children, their lovers. Of course. It was perfectly normal behavior. How else did anyone manage to get their backs oiled?

A child ran past calling loudly, 'Maman! Maman, *j'ai faim*!'

Gil gave a sharp start, as though he too had been in a trance and had woken up. His hands lifted. He stood up, took a tissue from the box of them she had got out of her beach bag, and slowly wiped his hands clean.

Still lying on her stomach, Bianca hurriedly pulled her swimsuit up, slipping the straps back over her oiled shoulders with shaky fingers. She was very flushed, breathing rapidly; she felt as if she had come up too fast from the bottom of the ocean and had bubbles of air in her blood.

'I'm going for a swim before we have to leave for the police station,' Gil said huskily.

'I'll sunbathe for a while.' She felt his brooding stare on her but stayed on her stomach, avoiding the need to meet his eyes.

'Don't stay out in the sun too much at first. English skin is meant for rain, not sunshine. Keep changing position.'

She heard him walking away and turned on to her back, sitting up to stare at the tall man making his way towards the sea.

There was a dazzle of light from the water, from the sky, which made the whole scene flicker, like a film shot through gauze; Gil's figure moved through it as if he were walking into infinity. His skin gleamed golden in the sunlight the way it had the first time she'd seen him. His body had a powerful male beauty—wide shoulders, a long, lean back, with that deep indentation in the middle of it, roughened by small dark hairs, slim hips and firm buttocks, long, muscled, dark-haired legs which moved easily, with grace.

Hunger ate at her. She lay down again and closed her eyes. The trouble was, she was really quite inexperienced with men. That sounded ridiculous when she had been married for years, and she had known Rob inside out, as well as she knew herself. Marriage to one man for many years made the two of you grow together, if it was a good marriage, and hers had been.

But knowing one man so well did not make you an expert on all men. She had never got to know any other men; she had been so young when she'd met Rob, and there hadn't been anyone else before she met him—and she had been totally faithful to him all through their life together; she was the faithful type, and had never felt the slightest temptation to look at anyone else. Rob's death had devastated her. She had thought she would never get over it.

Until now she would have sworn there would never be another man for her. She had always believed that love did not come to you twice—not love as strong and sure as she had felt for Rob.

But this isn't love! she thought angrily. She knew what the feeling was, and she was ashamed of it. Lust was an ugly word.

There were nicer words for it—desire, passion, infatuation. They were all basic instincts, physical responses—a matter of pure chemistry, of flesh, not spirit. They were illusions, in a sense, because she hardly knew the man; she had not even met him when she'd first felt this way. She had seen him almost naked and wanted him, wanted him with clamouring hunger.

Men were supposed to react that way, but not women—certainly not women like her. She was in many ways a conventional woman, with traditional responses and habits. She had followed a traditional path from girlhood—had married and had children, had stayed at home and looked after them and run the home, and had only gone into business when her husband died.

She was forty years old, a sensible, businesslike, down-to-earth woman—and Gil Marquez made her feel like a schoolgirl. Her body seemed unable to stop reacting to him. Her heart beating fast. Her breathing coming and going irregularly. Her nerves prickling, her skin burning.

I've got to stop it, she thought. I have to get over this. And to do that I must keep out of his way.

But how could she do that when she kept meeting him? Maybe she'd take a coach trip somewhere, she thought—it would be nice to go to Granada and see the Alhambra; that would be a fascinating trip; the Moorish architecture of the palace was so beautiful, and the gardens were said to be stunning. She would need a whole day there, would be out of the hotel for hours, and safe from meeting Gil—no doubt the hotel could make all the arrangements for her. That was part of their offered service—there were coach brochures on the reception desk in the hotel, she had noticed. Even if there was no trip to Granada tomorrow, there were lots of places to visit in this area. She was bound to find a coach trip to one of them.

'I think we'd better be on our way. It's gone half-past eleven. Are you ready?'

His voice made her jump, eyes wide, dark blue; she sat up, got to her feet, very flushed, quickly pulled her yellow cotton tunic dress over her head and collected her towel and other belongings a little clumsily because she was so aware of him standing there watching her. He made her intensely self-conscious.

'I'm ready. I must go back to my apartment first. I won't be more than five minutes.'

He walked with her to her apartment. 'I'll go and change too, then I'll collect my car from the hotel garage. Can you meet me outside the hotel in ten minutes?'

She nodded and hurried through her front door. Ten minutes would just give her time to shower rapidly, put on clean clothes and some make-up.

She made it to the hotel just in time; Gil's long, sleek car pulled up beside her as she arrived, and he leaned over to open the passenger door. She felt the assessing flick of his grey eyes as she climbed in beside him.

'That dress is exactly the colour of your eyes!' he murmured, and her pulses began their tormenting clamouring again.

She kept her gaze down, clicked her seatbelt home, then smoothed the skirt of her blue linen dress down over her knees as he drove away. Gil shot her another glance; out of the corner of her eye she saw his mouth indent ironically.

'Nervous?'

She stiffened. 'What about?'

'Identifying the guy who attacked you, of course,' he said softly. 'What did you think I meant?'

She ignored the last question and answered the first one, her voice husky but her chin determined. 'I'm not looking forward to the identification parade, but I'll go through with it. I was very scared last night; I'm angry about that. I wouldn't want anyone else to have that happen to them because I didn't help the police.'

They were in Marbella now; slowing at traffic lights, Gil gave her a sudden, brilliant smile. 'Bravo! You are right—next time he might attack a young girl or an old woman, and next time the knife might be used and someone might die.'

She shivered. 'I know. At the time I was reacting rather than thinking about what was happening... but afterwards, when I was in bed, I kept reliving the moment when he pulled the knife out and I'm only now beginning to realise just how terrified I was.'

'I expect you'll have panic attacks now and then for quite a while; it's only natural. Talking about it helps; you reduce the anxiety and the shock every time you talk it out with someone.'

He's a nice man, she thought with a pang. He's kind and thoughtful. But I'm going home in two weeks and we'll never meet again—and I'm too old for a holiday romance. I probably always was! I was never the type to throw myself into a brief affair, even before I married Rob. I'm far too conservative and cautious.

Scared! mocked a little voice inside her. You were always scared stiff of taking risks. You would never leap before you looked or gamble on your feelings.

He drew up outside a large police station and looked at his watch. 'Just on time; we'll have to hurry or they might think we aren't coming after all.'

The Spanish police were gravely kind and polite, but it was still as disturbing an experience, in a way, as the original attack. She had to look through a window at a line of men first. None of them looked familiar; they were mostly the same height, same build, and all wore blue jeans and a white T-shirt.

'I didn't see his face,' she pointed out. 'His helmet hid it.'

The policemen looked disappointed but unsurprised; they must have known the chances of her identifying the mugger were not good.

'Isn't anything about any of them familiar?' Gil asked her.

She looked helplessly at him. 'You saw him too—what do you think?'

He shrugged in wry regret. 'I didn't see him at close quarters; I just saw a shape, an outline, black leather and a motorbike helmet—nothing I could identify.'

The policeman with them said something in Spanish to Gil, who turned to her and quietly asked, 'Could you bear to walk along the line? They just want to know if this is the same man who attacked you. You might find something familiar, pick up a physical clue, a smell. They won't be able to use it in court, but it would still be useful to the police.'

She swallowed, then nodded. 'OK.'

She walked slowly, looking at each face, each man's shape, trying not to tremble visibly although her insides were quaking like jelly and she felt sick. When she reached the end of the line she knew she had not recognised anyone, but she tried again, this time not looking at their faces, just staring downwards as if trying to recognise their feet.

At one point she paused, drawing a sharp breath, her nostrils quivering as they picked up the scent of sweat, of garlic, of something less identifiable but definite—the scent of fear.

She looked up into black eyes and knew it was him. At that instant she remembered the moment when he had drawn the knife and she saw his black-gloved hand, the cuff of his black leather jacket...and the slight gap between them.

The scar. She looked down at his hand, reached for it.

He tried to pull away from her. The policeman beside her spoke sharply to him in Spanish, and the boy reluctantly let her lift his hand, push back the cuff of his jacket.

The red scar was there. She let his hand fall, and then, as she had been instructed, she tapped him on the shoulder. His eyes hated her, threatened her; she sensed the tension of his stiffening muscles as if he was going to hit her. He spat out Spanish under his breath, words she didn't understand but whose meaning she guessed without difficulty.

He would like to kill her. He wished he had used that knife on her in the street last night.

The policeman at the end of the line came quickly forward to escort her safely out of the white-washed room.

'It's definitely him,' she said shakily, and explained about the knife-cut on the boy's wrist.

'You never mentioned it before,' Gil said, frowning.

'I only remembered it when I saw him again.' She was shaking now.

Gil moved closer, put an arm around her, his eyes focusing on her white face.

'Are you OK? Come and sit down.'

She would have liked to leave then, go back to her apartment and lie down on her bed alone, but she had to go through the further ordeal of answering questions about the incident. Gil translated for her, his chair right next to hers. The language gap made the long session even more difficult to handle; she was glad of the glass of water that Gil requested, and got, for her, but she was even more grateful when the policeman finally asked her to sign her statement and let her leave.

'Was my identification any real help?' she asked him through Gil, and the other man shrugged, his face wry.

'As you did not see his face, I am afraid it was little help to us, and although you say you saw the cut on his wrist during the incident you never mentioned it in your first statement; but at least you have confirmed our belief that it was the same person who attacked you and the others.'

'So I did pick out the boy you had arrested for the other attack?'

The policeman nodded, his face unreadable.

'What will happen to him now?' she rather nervously asked, hoping he would not be released on bail while she was in Spain.

Again the policeman shrugged. 'We will hold him while we are making further enquiries. The man they mugged last night has recovered consciousness, but the hospital will not let us talk to him because he is still in a state of shock. Once he is well enough to see us we'll know whether or not we have a good case against the two men we picked up.'

'Well, good luck,' she said, shaking hands, and the policeman gave her a warm smile.

'Enjoy the rest of your holiday. But remember, we may need you to appear in court some time in the future.'

What if they had to release those two men for lack of evidence? she thought as they drove back towards the hotel. She remembered the hatred in the eyes of the man she had picked out in the identity parade; he had wanted to kill her. A shiver of fear ran down her back.

Gil shot her a sideways look, his grey eyes piercing as they assessed her expression.

'You are quite safe inside the hotel grounds, you know,' he said gently.

She gave him a startled glance. How had he known what she was thinking?

He said quietly, 'Our security system is foolproof. No one without identification can move about inside the grounds without being picked up on our hidden cameras or by our security patrols.'

Her mind knew, rationally, that if she was sensible and did not go wandering around the town late at night again she was perfectly safe.

Why didn't she feel safe, then? Why was she on edge now, in broad daylight, in the safety of Gil's car?

CHAPTER FOUR

'I WOULD like to have lunch with you,' Gil said as they drew up outside the hotel, and Bianca opened her mouth to refuse, but before she could say anything he added, 'Unfortunately, I must get back to work. My assistant is standing in for me and I have to take over from him. But will you have dinner with me tonight?'

'I'm sorry,' she said stiffly. 'I would like to get an early night, and eating a heavy meal in the evening always gives me indigestion.'

'That's because you aren't used to it. In Spain we always eat late at night, rarely before nine—and our meals are quite heavy, but we don't get indigestion.'

'I don't know how you ever manage to get any sleep when you start eating at nine or ten o'clock at night!'

'We have our siesta during the afternoon; we don't need to get in eight hours during the night. Going to bed in the heat of the day is a very civilised way of dealing with our climate—you should try it. We must convert you to our ways while you're here.'

Somehow his gaze made her nerves prickle—she wasn't altogether sure he was talking about sleeping. Those grey eyes had a mocking amusement in them that disturbed her.

She looked away, said hurriedly, 'Well, I'll skip dinner altogether and just have a light supper in my apartment. I must do some shopping, get some fresh food from the hotel shop. I haven't been there yet—does it sell salads and cold meats?'

67

'It is a mini-supermarket—it carries a very wide range of goods, and I'm sure you'll find what you want, but if you don't you only have to ask and we'll get it for you within twenty-four hours.'

'I'll remember that,' she said as he came round to open the door for her and help her out. 'And thank you for being so kind and helpful, Señor Marquez——'

'Gil,' he interrupted. 'We know each other well enough now to use first names, don't we, Bianca?'

Their eyes met and she drew a shaky breath, somehow managed to say huskily, 'It was very good of you to take me to the police station and interpret for me, Gil. I'm very grateful.'

'Then have dinner with me tomorrow; I've invited Freddie and Karl to dinner—a foursome is much more enjoyable—and you do like them, don't you?'

'Yes, very much,' she said, relieved, breaking into a smile. If they were going to be there she needn't feel alarmed about being alone with him. She had liked Freddie the minute they met; she would enjoy getting to know her better.

Gil's eyes watched her with irony as if he knew what she was thinking, but his voice was level and calm. 'So you'll change your mind and join us? We'll eat early, at eight, just for you! The kitchen can cope with that—they're used to English visitors wanting to eat at unreasonable hours.'

She laughed. 'It's hard to change the habit of a lifetime, you know.'

He looked down at her, a tall man with a brooding authority, his eyes holding hers.

'Changing is what life is all about, Bianca. We do it all the time, minute by minute, day by day, year by year, so gradually that we barely notice. How many times have

ou met someone you knew ten years ago and been
mazed by how much they've changed in those years?'
Ie paused, then said quietly, 'You can't fight time or
fe, Bianca. You can't stop the clock, or turn it back.'

She felt a surge of the angry, passionate regret she had
elt ever since Rob died.

'Life isn't fair!' she broke out and Gil's mouth twisted
rryly.

'Who promised it would be? It's time you grew up,
Bianca!'

That made her laugh. 'I'm forty years old!' The ad-
nission almost took her breath away. Her age was some-
hing else she angrily resisted.

Gil grinned. 'And here I am lecturing you when I'm
wo years younger!'

'Only two?' she retorted, but was quite relieved be-
ause she had suspected that he might only be thirty-
ive or so.

'Thanks for the compliment,' he said, his eyes
leaming. 'You look much younger than forty yourself.'

They were standing in the hotel lobby now. The re-
eptionist waved urgently at Gil, who nodded back at
er then looked down at Bianca. 'I must go. If you have
ny problems at all ring my office and I'll deal with them.
And stay in the hotel grounds for the rest of the day.'

She prickled, resenting the autocratic tone.

'Don't give me orders, Señor Marquez!'

His eyes were sardonic. 'Don't be stupid, Bianca. I'm
ot giving you orders, I'm advising you, for your own
ood, to stay where you can be protected. And my name
; Gil. Remember?'

He held out his hand and courtesy demanded that she
ake it. Slowly and unwillingly she held out her own hand

but he did not shake it. He lifted her hand to his mouth
and kissed the back of it formally, with a slight bow.

She drew a startled breath. He straightened, looking
down into her startled eyes.

'Take a siesta after lunch, Bianca. Start living like a
Spaniard—go to bed in the afternoon. Let us teach you
how to enjoy life.'

She knew she was turning pink and saw that it amused
him; his eyes teased her, but as he stopped speaking he
released her hand, turned and walked away towards the
reception desk.

Bianca hurriedly turned away too and went into the
dining-room where they were still serving a buffet lunch.
A waiter came to show her to a table and ask if she
would want some wine with her meal.

For once, she decided, she would; the morning had
been exhausting and after lunch she would take Gil's
advice and go to bed for an afternoon siesta.

'A half-carafe of your house white, please, and some
mineral water.'

When the waiter had gone she went over to the buffet,
collected a plate and began to wander around choosing
from the food. By now the selection was not as extensive
as it no doubt had been at the start of lunchtime—the
other guests had plundered the plates and left only scraps
of the most popular food. Bianca wasn't very hungry,
however; she chose salad and a small slice of cold
poached salmon.

As she went back to her table to begin eating she suddenly saw someone waving from a table at the far side
of the room, by the window.

Breaking into a smile, she recognised Freddie and went
over there, carrying her plate. Freddie was chic and eye-
riveting in a very plain white lawn dress which made her

tan more marked; she glittered, too, with gold—small, shield-shaped earrings in her ears, a chunky gold bracelet on her arm, a thin chain around her neck. The simplicity and yet richness of the ensemble worked so well together that you would have supposed it to have been designed as a whole by whoever had made the dress, thought Bianca, whose business was fashion, but she suspected that Freddie herself had chosen the jewellery to match the expensively simple white dress. Freddie had a natural style which money could not buy.

She smiled warmly at Bianca, asking, 'How are you today?' Her eyes searched Bianca's face. 'You look pale, and no wonder! Gil told us what happened last night in Marbella—it must have been terrifying. For such a thing to happen... it could ruin your holiday—how lucky Gil came along when he did.'

Bianca nodded. 'Yes, it was very lucky.' Even if she wished it had been someone else she was grateful that he had arrived when he did. 'At least I wasn't hurt, and didn't lose anything! It could have been so much worse. I've just had to go to a police station for an identity parade—that was quite scary, too; I hated doing it.'

'Did you pick anyone out?'

'I didn't recognise anyone, but I did feel sure that one man was the mugger; I pointed him out to the police and they said he was one of the men they had picked up. The other man stayed on the bike during the attack, and I never even noticed him.'

Freddie looked puzzled. 'If you didn't recognise him how could you pick him out?'

'There was something... I don't know, I just felt sure it was him; it was instinctive, a sort of sixth sense, and I might have decided I was wrong, but then I looked in his eyes and...he hated me...' Bianca shivered, remembering that moment, and Freddie looked horrified.

'How terrible! You poor thing!'

'Let's not talk about it,' said Bianca hurriedly. 'I just want to forget about it, now all that's over.' She looked at the other places at the table. 'Where's your family? Have they eaten and left?'

'Karl took them sailing. Gil has a yacht moored at Puerto Jose Banus...'

'Where?'

'That's a marina, just down the coast from here, at Nueva Andalucía; they have mooring for hundreds of yachts, a casino and a leisure complex with bars and nightclubs and restaurants...and swimming-pools—they have several of those, too. It's a fun place and Karl and the children loved it the minute they saw it. It's their sort of place.'

Bianca saw the waiter coming back with her carafe of wine. 'Well, I'd better go back to my own table.'

Freddie glanced across the room. 'Are you alone too?'

Bianca nodded.

'Well, then, will you join me? I've had my meal, but I'm going to have some coffee. It would be nice to have some company.'

'I'd love to,' Bianca said, sitting down opposite her. She looked round to wave at the waiter. He had already noticed her change of place, and came over at once with her wine. 'Thank you,' she said, smiling at him, and he gave her a polite, grave bow.

'Will you have some of this?' Bianca asked Freddie who shook her head, smiling.

'I had a glass with my lunch, thank you; that's more than enough for me. I get a headache if I drink much wine in the middle of the day.' She gestured at Bianca's plate. 'Do eat your lunch. Ah, here comes my coffee.'

Bianca began to eat her poached salmon, which was dressed with hollandaise sauce, beautifully made, smooth and cool with a light lemon flavour. It was the perfect accompaniment to the fresh, crisp salad to which she had added a spoon of home-made vinaigrette at the buffet table.

Freddie sipped her coffee and sighed. 'Ah, I do love good coffee, and they know how to make it here! That's Gil, of course—he insists on his kitchens turning out good coffee as well as the best possible food.'

'Has he always worked in hotels?'

Freddie looked up and grinned at her. 'His family have been in the hotel business for generations; he trained in some of the best hotels in Europe. It came naturally to him, the business. He is like all hoteliers—a fanatic about detail. They have to be. Nothing escapes Gil's eye; he notices everything. He had a hotel in Madrid when he met my sister but he sold it after their divorce, bought this place and moved down here.'

'He owns this hotel?'

Nodding, Freddie said, 'He wanted a change of scene. He's not a man who likes to fail, and the failure of their marriage depressed him for a long time. For the first couple of years he was very angry, but I'm glad to find he is over that now. He has realised that Mady was the wrong woman for him—and he was the wrong man for her. Their divorce was inevitable, and you can't fight inevitability.'

'Is she happy with her second husband?' asked Bianca, remembering what Gil had told her about the German millionaire his ex-wife had chosen.

'Oh, idyllic.' Freddie met her incredulous eyes and gave her a dry, amused smile. 'Yes, I am serious! Gil has told you about them? Look, I love Gil, Karl and I are most fond of him, but he is bitter about Mady now. She hurt him, he is over it now, but it has left him cynical about her; he is hard towards her. OK, you can understand it—he is a man, very much a man, and Mady behaved badly to him—but still, do not believe everything he says about my sister.'

'I imagine divorce does warp the way someone feels about their ex-partner,' Bianca murmured, pushing away her plate as she tired of her salad. She felt curiously depressed herself. When Gil had talked about his ex-wife he had not sounded as if his heart was broken, but what Freddie had said made sense. Mady had hurt him when she'd left him. Maybe under the cynicism he still loved her? He must have done once or he would never have married her in the first place, and love didn't die just because someone walked out on you. Or died, she thought, suppressing a sigh.

Gil Marquez did not give her the impression of being the sort of man who recovered easily or quickly from a wound like that, any more than she had. She, of all people, knew what it felt like—she still missed Rob every day. His absence from her life was like a hole in the heart. Was that how it was for Gil?

'Mady was wise to get out of a marriage that had been a mistake,' said Freddie flatly. 'Gil believes she left him because she wanted a richer man, but it is not true. Oh, Gustav is very, very rich, but that is not why Mady needed him. Gustav is old enough to be her father—that is true too—she is thirty, Gustav is sixty-five and already has two sons who are older than Mady. It is easy to see why Gil is cynical about what happened, but he does not see them together. Gustav makes her happy; he takes care of her, looks after her.'

Frowning, Bianca said, 'I'd have said Gil was the sort of man to do that too.'

Freddie shrugged, spread her hands and leaned towards Bianca. 'In some ways, that's true, but...Mady was the last child my parents had, you see. They adored her, and they spoiled her—we all did—and in some ways she is still a little girl. Mady is not very bright, not strong-minded—oh, she is not mentally retarded, but she is childish, to be honest. Spoilt and childish, but she can be very sweet, and she is beautiful. She made a big mistake marrying Gil. They got married too quickly, before they knew each other. They both soon realised it was not working, but Gil probably wouldn't have given up so soon; he is the sort of man who hates to admit a mistake; he would have gone on trying to change her, make her into the sort of wife he wanted and needed. He never asked himself what Mady wanted and needed. Gil scared her, made her feel inadequate; she got more and more unhappy.'

'You're making Gil sound very unlikeable,' Bianca commented slowly, frowning.

'No, no, I'm very fond of Gil—it wasn't his fault any more than it was Mady's. It was just a mistake for both of them. Luckily Mady met Gustav and ran away with him, and ever since she has been happy.'

'Is he?' asked Bianca drily. It sounded such an odd marriage—a spoilt young woman and a man old enough to be her father!

'Gustav? Very happy; he's proud of having a beautiful young wife, and he enjoys taking care of her, spoiling her. He never had a daughter, only two sons—I think

Mady is the daughter he never had, and far more than that. He really loves her.'

'Didn't Gil?'

Bianca felt almost angry on Gil's behalf—Freddie had just said that Gil had been hurt, so he must have loved his wife, and it must have been humiliating to lose a wife to a man old enough to be her father. People had probably laughed at Gil behind his back—they wouldn't dare laugh at him face to face. He must have been very angry for a long time; she had picked up the echoes of that anger when he'd spoken to her about his wife and her new husband.

Freddie gave her a searching glance as if guessing that Gil must have talked about her sister. 'Yes, of course he thought he did,' she said defensively. 'But I don't think he ever really knew her. The Mady he fell in love with didn't exist. You see, Mady is beautiful and she has style, she knows how to dress, she looks sophisticated and worldly-wise, but she isn't. He thought what he saw was what Mady was like, but he didn't know enough about her, and he never really understood her. You see, she has the mind and heart of a child, a very vain child; she spends a lot of time in front of her mirror, she loves clothes and jewellery, anything that makes her look even prettier, but she is never spiteful or mean; she has a sweet nature, she is kind, and loving to anyone who is loving to her. It is just that you cannot expect her to be an adult; you can never lean on Mady or rely on her.'

'You can't blame Gil for feeling cheated,' protested Bianca. 'Didn't he only want what most men want from a wife? It was certainly what Rob...what my husband expected from me—a partner to share life with, have children with...'

'I know,' said Freddie, smiling with faint sadness. 'I know it's what Karl expects. But then I am not my sister. Mady can't help being the way she is—there is something missing in poor little Mady; she is stuck at about twelve years old. Lucky for her that she finally met the perfect man for her: Gustav adores her.'

'And what do his sons think of her?'

'They love her too. Oh, if she tried to take their mother's place they might have resented her, but Mady never could, never thought of trying. They can see that she's genuinely sweet and rather helpless. They're pleased that their father has someone in his life, someone to look after. Gustav is the sort of man who likes to take care of people.'

'Are his sons married?'

Freddie gave her a dry look. 'You're so sharp! No, neither of them is married yet. If they were, it might be another story.'

'I expect it would be, if Gustav is very rich,' said Bianca. 'If his sons had wives and children of their own, I imagine they would be afraid that your sister might have children. Then Gustav would probably leave some of his money to his new family. Money is what families usually quarrel about.'

'I'm sure you're right,' agreed Freddie, laughing. 'You are good about human nature, aren't you? But I don't think Mady will ever have a baby. I know she doesn't want one. Oh, she likes children, but she is too much a child herself; she couldn't take the responsibility of having a baby.'

The more she heard about Mady, the more Bianca sympathised with Gil; his marriage must have been a disaster. She could not imagine him being happy with a wife like that.

After lunch she and Freddie walked back through the gardens together and parted outside Bianca's apartment. She was glad to notice a security man in a blue uniform walking past them on the path; it made her feel safer.

She closed her shutters, took off her dress and, wearing only her bra and panties and a thin silk slip, lay down on her bed in the shadowy half-light. Outside birds called in the trees; there was the far-off sound of the sea, and children's voices as they played on the beach. Bianca lay still, listening, trying not to think; she had barely slept last night and was mentally and emotionally exhausted; sleep crept up on her within minutes.

She called in at the reception desk later that afternoon and booked herself on a coach trip to Granada and the Alhambra Palace the following day, then she walked over to the hotel shop and bought a range of food—salad, eggs, cheese, fruit, bread, coffee and tea, breakfast cereal, orange juice and marmalade. She carried two heavy shopping bags back to her apartment and put all her purchases away, reflecting that she had no need to eat in the hotel dining-room for some days now. She could have light meals in her own apartment and keep out of Gil's way. She hadn't wanted to cook while she was here on holiday, but preparing a salad was no problem.

That evening she ate a boiled egg with toast followed by some fruit, and went to bed early. In spite of having had a siesta that afternoon she slept well; she must have been even more tired than she realised.

She woke very early, though, and showered, dressed in a full, flared dark green cotton skirt and a very pale green T-shirt, put sandals on her bare feet, brushed her hair and put on a light make-up, then ate breakfast on her balcony in a pale primrose light. The early morning was cool, the birds calling as they flew from tree to tree across the hotel grounds, the black shadows of cypress and cedar diminishing as the sun rose higher, the blue sea veiled in a haze of mist. A few people came out to swim in the pool below her apartment and she watched them dreamily, deciding she would get up early tomorrow morning and swim there herself.

At eight-thirty she was on a coach *en route* to Granada through the Sierra Nevada, the mountains rising behind the coastal strip of the Costa del Sol. The road through the dramatic, rough grey slopes of the bare mountains was tortuous, winding, often badly maintained. Bianca's heart was in her mouth as they climbed higher and higher, sometimes so close to the edge that she found herself looking down into steep, plunging valleys, the coach turning a bend so sharp that the end of it would stick out over the edge. Several times she just shut her eyes, tensely twisting her fingers together, and prayed.

The Alhambra stood on a mountain overlooking the city of Granada. It was an enormous complex set in magnificent gardens known as the Generalife.

Both fortress and palace, a place of power and strength, but of beauty too, the Alhambra was the home of the Nasrid royal family, Islamic kings who fought the Spanish Christians throughout the thirteenth century. The Moorish palace was a maze of courtyards and rooms, austerely sensuous, rich with mosaic arches and walls—geometric designs where every single shape had a symbolic meaning...this wavy line water, that triangle a tree...their colours often as bright as day because the tiny stones set in the mosaic had not faded with time—they were pin-sharp. Stone fountains in the courtyards filled the air with the sound of water, flowers in the gardens scented the morning, great stone columns and windows filtered misty light into the shadowy rooms where once beautiful women had lain on silken cushions, bathed together, sung, or men fiercely argued for peace or war, or haggled over trade. They were all silent now, and empty, those great echoing rooms, except when the tide of tourists washed through them during daylight hours.

Bianca wandered dreamily after the coach party, half listening to their guide, her eyes and ears intent on the beauty of everything she saw and heard, both in the palace and in the gardens, with their spring flowers and scented roses and the great black shadows of the cedars and cypress trees.

She was one of the first to emerge through the gates and walk down towards the hotel coach.

As she wandered over the broken cobbles she heard a motorbike engine idling, and started. She looked around the crowded car park and saw the bike at once—two men sat on it, both in black leather, both wearing helmets with black glass in the visor, which hid their faces. She couldn't see their eyes, yet she was certain they were staring at her.

Bianca stopped dead, her nerves jumping. She knew that the men who had attacked her were safely locked up, back in Marbella, many miles away—it couldn't be the same men.

All the same, she couldn't move; she was paralysed for a minute, her blood beating in her ear. As she stared, the rider kick-started the motorbike and it roared into life and shot forward, straight for her.

Bianca turned to run back up the hill towards the Alhambra, and met a group of her fellow passengers from the coach coming downwards. They stared at her, exclaiming.

'Are you all right?' asked a middle-aged man she had seen get on the coach at the hotel.

'She's as white as a ghost,' his wife said in a soft Scottish accent. 'Aren't you well, dear?'

The motorbike swerved away and the male passenger stared after it, then looked at Bianca. 'Was it them? Did they try to grab your bag? That happened the other night, you know; one of our people from the hotel was mugged in Marbella. That's their technique ... they ride around town on motorbikes and snatch handbags from tourists.'

Bianca mumbled something. 'I thought they might ... Stupid of me, but I was nervous.'

'I don't blame you,' said the Scottish woman. 'You never know, do you, these days? You're not safe anywhere.'

Bianca shivered.

'You're scaring the life out of her!' scolded the man. 'Come along, my dear; get into the coach; you need to sit down quietly for a while.'

She gratefully sank into the front seat on the coach. Leaning back, she closed her eyes, waiting for the coach to drive back down the mountain to Granada itself.

Of course it had not been the same two men on the motorbike; it was just a coincidence. All the same, the shock still reverberated through her.

The coach finally set off and bumped down winding, traffic-filled roads until it reached the city, where everyone climbed out again to filter into a large Spanish restaurant with traditional wood flooring and heavy oak furniture.

People immediately rushed off to use the lavatories; Bianca had been first off the coach and was therefore first in the queue. The tour of the Alhambra had been tiring; her skin was damp with perspiration after all that walking and then the shock of seeing the men on the motorbike. As well as wanting to use the lavatory she was dying to wash her hands and face.

The ladies' powder-room was not simply clean and modern, it was beautifully decorated, with blue and yellow traditional Spanish designs on white tiles, yellow basins and dark wood everywhere.

She washed her hands and face, sighing with pleasure at the splash of cold water on her hot, dusty skin. She combed her hair, put on a little lipstick, a film of foundation, dusted powder over her skin, then went back into the restaurant, stopping in her tracks in disbelief as she saw Gil.

She almost thought she was seeing things for a minute; that she had conjured him up; he was a figment of her imagination.

But if she had imagined him would she have dressed him in a smooth dark suit of formal cut and design, with a stiff white shirt and pale grey tie?

That was what he was wearing, anyway—and he was really there; he wasn't a dream. He was sitting at a table, talking to the guide who had shown them round the Alhambra.

He saw her a second later; he smiled and she felt her heart pause in its beating. Involuntarily she smiled back, then was frightened by the depth of her pleasure at seeing him. This was madness; she had only known the man a couple of days. Why was she so happy suddenly that she could almost burst into song like a bird?

Oh, grow up! she told herself angrily.

Gil got up and walked away from the guide towards her; she moved towards him as if pulled on a rope, helpless to fight that tug of inevitability. They met in the middle of the large restaurant and she felt as if they were alone in an empty landscape. The other people around them, the room itself, dissolved, and there was only her and Gil. Nothing else existed.

Looking down at her, he said, 'I thought you agreed that you wouldn't leave the hotel grounds for the next day or two?'

The accusing tone made her stiffen resentfully. 'I am on holiday! I wanted to see something of this part of Spain, and I thought I'd be safe enough on a coach trip so long as I made sure I was never left alone. This time I kept with everyone else wherever we went.'

'At least you've had that much sense!' he muttered, frowning darkly.

'Well, the police have got those two men locked up; I'm in no danger, am I?' Bianca said. 'What are you doing here, anyway? You didn't follow just because you found out I had come on this coach trip?'

His face was tense, sombre. 'No. I came because the police rang me to say that they have had to release the two muggers.'

CHAPTER FIVE

BIANCA'S face paled. 'I knew it! I thought I was imagining things, but all the time my unconscious was right—it was him!'

'What are you talking about?' Gil stared at her, frowning.

Huskily she told him. 'While we were coming out of the Alhambra, I saw two men on a motorbike sitting watching the gates. I was walking on my own, in front of the others, and the bike suddenly started and drove straight at me. It was deliberate—and it was them! I knew it was, the minute I saw them; I panicked—I turned round and ran back towards the rest of the coach party, who weren't far behind me, and then they swerved away and drove off.'

Gil stared down at her, his mouth a hard white line. 'You were doing it again, weren't you? Walking on your own, not staying with the rest of the group... you stupid woman, don't you ever learn? What did I say to you? You should never have come on this trip. If you wanted to go to the Alhambra I'd have taken you.'

His voice had risen; she felt a stir, saw the other people from the coach turn to stare curiously at them as they took their places around the prepared lunch tables.

'Shh...' she urged, glaring at him. 'Everyone's listening!' Waiters had begun to bring out huge tureens, and they moved around the tables ladling soup into the bowl in front of each guest. 'They're serving lunch—I must go!' She moved to walk away and he caught her

arm; she looked angrily down at his long fingers encir-
cling her flesh. 'Let go of me!'

He released her with an impatient little grunt. 'Just
tell me this—what made you think it was them? How
could they know you were here, anyway?'

She looked down, biting her lower lip, and thought
aloud. 'Yes, how did they know? We left so early in the
morning—if they were only released today, how could
they know where to find me? Unless...' She looked up
at Gil and his face was dark with anger.

'Unless someone at the hotel told them! I was beginning to realise that myself. How else could they have
known you had gone to Granada?'

'I suppose they could have rung the hotel, asked for
me, and been told where I was?'

'That's strictly against my rules,' he bit out through
his teeth, frowning. 'We have a lot of famous people
staying with us—no personal information is ever supposed to be given out. But I'll check on that as soon as
I get back. If that is what happened, it won't happen
again.'

Bianca was sorry for any member of the staff who had
given out the information. She wouldn't like to have to
face Gil in this mood. He was dressed so smoothly and
formally, in that dark suit, with the pale grey tie and
white shirt—but danger radiated out of him.

The Spanish guide came over to them and gave Gil
an obsequious smile. 'Señor Marquez...you are going
to eat with us? The soup is being served now. I have
kept a place for you beside me, and for the señora, of
course.'

Gil gave him an abstracted glance, then nodded, as if
suddenly realising what the man had said. 'Oh, yes—
yes, of course.' He put his hand under Bianca's elbow

and guided her towards the table. 'I expect you're hungry,' he said to her. 'Sightseeing is tiring and it's a long time since you had breakfast, isn't it?'

'I'm starving,' she admitted as he pulled back her chair to allow her to sit down. Everyone else at the table had already been served and had begun to drink their soup, a smooth tomato with strips of roasted red pepper floating on the surface.

'This looks unusual,' Bianca said, picking up her spoon.

'*Crema sevillana*,' the guide told her, sitting down on one side of her while Gil took the chair on the other. 'A traditional dish from Seville.'

The waiter leaned over her shoulder. '*Pan*?'

She looked up, startled. 'Sorry?' Then she saw the wicker basket of bread he offered her and took a piece, smiling. 'Oh, yes, thank you.'

'Time you learnt some Spanish,' Gil said, taking some of the domed, golden bread. '*Vino*?' He picked up a carafe of red wine, offering it to her, but she shook her head.

'Just water, thank you.'

'*Agua*,' he said clearly. 'Say it—*agua*.'

'*Agua*,' she said with a touch of resentment because the people around them were listening and smiling. 'I knew *agua* was water; I just find it hard to use my little bit of Spanish when anyone is listening.'

'We appreciate if it you do,' he said drily. 'Try your soup.'

She bristled at his commanding tone, but took a spoonful of the soup, noting a touch of onion or garlic in the flavour; it was very good, and so was the bread but then she was so hungry, she would have enjoyed almost anything she ate.

'Delicious,' she said, and Gil smiled at her, suddenly relaxing, his grey eyes very light in that darkly tanned face. She felt her heart skip a beat and looked hurriedly down again, taking more soup.

'So, what did you think of the Alhambra?' Gil asked in a conversational tone.

'It was a dream! I loved the colours of the mosaics on the walls, all those courtyards and fountains. I would have liked it even more if I'd been there alone, I expect—it was so crowded and we were moved on all the time from room to room—it was hard to feel the atmosphere.'

'Tourism kills the thing it comes to see,' agreed Gil, leaning back in his chair, his soup finished. 'But everyone deserves to see something like the Alhambra—you can learn so much from a place where people have lived long ago; it teaches a very healthy respect for the culture of those Moors who lived in this part of Spain. They were brilliant architects and builders, poets in the way they created such beauty from mere brick and stone. They weren't even allowed, by their religion, to reproduce the human form; they had to rely on colour and geometric shape.'

'I know very little about the history of Spain,' she said as the waiter appeared and took their plates away.

'I'll find you a book to read.'

She opened her mouth to remind him that she couldn't read Spanish, but he gave her a wry smile, his eyes mocking.

'In English,' he promised, and she thought, I'm going to take Spanish lessons when I get home! Next time I come to Spain I'll make sure I can speak to people here in their own language.

The soup was followed by a chicken casserole, the golden meat sprinkled with almonds. Served with saffron-flavoured rice, this too had a strong taste of garlic, and of herbs too, although she couldn't identify which had been used.

'What's this called?' she asked Gil, who told her.

'*Pollo en pepitoria.*'

'*Pollo* is chicken?'

He nodded, amused. 'You're beginning to pick up a few scraps of Spanish, you see?'

She gave him a dry look and he laughed.

Ice-cream followed the chicken, whipped white clouds of it, sprinkled with chopped nuts and cherries.

'*Helado,*' Gil translated for her.

'*Helado,*' she repeated, and the waiter grinned down at her.

While they were drinking their coffee, Gil murmured to her in a voice low enough not to be overheard by the others, 'You're coming back with me, not going on the coach.'

Flushed, she shook her head. 'I'll go with the others!'

Coolly, he insisted, 'We need to talk about what happened; I think the police should be informed at once.'

She looked at him uneasily. 'But I've no proof that the men on that motorbike were the same two who attacked me!'

'The bike drove straight at you, you said!'

She nodded. 'It did. I'm quite certain about that— they stared at me first, from a distance, then the bike began to move and came very fast. If I hadn't moved, they would have hit me.'

'But they swerved away when you ran back to the rest of your group?'

'That's right.' She remembered it, shivering. 'I really thought they were going to plough into me. At the time I was certain it was the same two—although I thought

they were still in custody. I just felt it was them and that
they were going to attack me. But I didn't see their faces
this time either. I have no evidence at all that it was the
same two men, and anyway, nothing happened. What
on earth is the point of going to the police?'

His mouth twisted. 'OK, if you don't want to talk to
the police you don't have to—but I'll ring them to find
out what time they released the two boys. If they couldn't
have got to Granada in time we'll know it wasn't them.
But just in case it was them you have got to be doubly
careful in future. You must not go out of the hotel
grounds, even on coach trips. If you want to sightsee or
shop, I'll take you, or make sure you're with someone
I trust. Freddie and Karl, for instance—Karl would take
good care of you. But if you were with a big group it
would be far too easy for someone to attack you and
get away.'

'I don't want to see the police again,' she confessed,
sighing. Her life back in England had always been so
quiet and tranquil; she wasn't used to coping with situations like this; she had felt on edge almost since she got
here and it seemed to get worse every day. 'Anyway, what
could they do?' she said. 'Nothing happened. I wasn't
attacked, I just thought I was going to be, and I could
simply have over-reacted; there could have been no threat
to me at all.'

He nodded. 'You could have done, but I somehow
don't think so. I don't see you as the over-imaginative
type.'

She wasn't so sure that was a compliment. What did
he mean by that?

'I think your instincts are pretty sound,' he went on,
and again she wondered exactly what he meant—was
there a mocking undertone to that, or was she being too

sensitive? He smiled drily at her. 'But, if it bothers you, OK, we won't tell the police about it...yet—we'll wait and see if they turn up again, but from now on you must be on your guard, keep your eyes open everywhere you go.' He looked down into her eyes insistently, and she noticed the faint little flecks of gold around the black pupil, like rays around a dark sun, so striking against the pale, pale colour of the iris.

Her voice husky, she murmured, 'Yes, don't worry, I certainly will.'

He was endlessly watchable, she thought. She couldn't stop looking at him: that golden skin, smooth and deeply tanned, with few lines on his face, only faint ones around his mouth and eyes, etched by smiling; the powerful structure of the bones beneath that skin; the thick, midnight-black hair; the wide, warm mouth, which had such charm when he smiled; the stubborn jawline.

The dark suit gave him a formal, conventional look, but Gil Marquez was neither formal nor conventional. The power he exuded was very different, a warm and physical power based on the body under those clothes, and with that a devastating self-assurance; no woman could ignore it, certainly not Bianca. Every nerve-end in her body was aware of him; he made her blood move faster, her breathing quicken, perspiration spring out on her hot skin.

He drove her back to Marbella shortly after that. He was driving a different car today, she noticed, settling into the front passenger seat of a sleek white sports car. The upholstery was black leather, deep and luxurious; the woodwork was golden, highly polished. Bianca knew nothing about cars, and she had no idea what make this one was, but she could see that it must have cost a fortune; Tom would love it; her son was crazy about cars, particularly special cars like this one.

She felt the curious stares of the other passengers, climbing up into their coach a few feet away, as she and Gil drove off. No doubt they wondered why she had left the tour party—but while the women stared at Gil the men were all envying his car, studying the lines of it and the speed with which it took off through Granada.

'Have you sold your other car?' she asked him, and he started, then shook his head, laughing.

'That's my business car; I use it for work—it's solid and conventional and gives me the right image. Image is everything in my business; the hotel has to breathe an air of luxury and at the same time be totally safe for our wealthy clients—so the car I drive when I'm at work has to be expensive but very safety-conscious, energy-conserving, solidly built, reassuring. When I'm not working I can do as I please, though, and this car is my private fantasy, my dream car. I expect some people would say it was my ego-booster, and maybe it is. I don't spend too much time analysing my unconscious. I have always wanted a fast sports car so as soon as I could afford one I bought this. It costs an arm and a leg to run, eats up petrol, and it seems to spend a lot of time in the garage being tuned up, but I love driving it.'

'I'm not surprised—my son would love it too,' she said, smiling. 'He's crazy about cars.'

'How old is he?'

'Fifteen.'

He gave her a sideways glance, his mouth twisting. 'A difficult age for boys—that's when they start arguing over everything they're told to do and being bloody-minded—is he at the problem stage?'

She made a little face. 'Not exactly; he can be annoying at times…untidy, reluctant to do anything—you know what teenagers are like—but he's a good boy at heart; he doesn't give me any real trouble.'

He shot her an amused look. 'Mothers always think their sons are wonderful, don't they?'

'Did yours?'

He smiled without looking at her this time, his eyes on the road. 'She had waited so long to get me, having girl after girl, she would have thought I was wonderful if I'd had two heads!'

'Is she still alive?' she asked, remembering that he had told her his father was dead.

'Yes—she's nearly eighty now, of course, but still very active. She lives in Madrid with my eldest sister, Gisela. My mother's a doting grandmother and Gisela has four children for her to spoil. She comes here to stay for a few weeks every year, for a holiday by the sea—usually in January, because Madrid is very cold in winter and Mamá hates cold weather. She visits my other sisters, too; we're scattered all over Spain—Eva is in Barcelona and Rosa lives near Alicante, so my mother goes on to Rosa from here every year. That's where she is right now. She will be going back to Madrid in a fortnight.'

'You sound like a very close family.'

'We are. Family is very important to us.' He glanced at her again. 'It's important to you too, isn't it?'

She nodded.

'What are your children's names?'

'My son's Thomas—we call him Tom; I must tell him about your car when I get home—he'll be fascinated. What sort of car is this?'

'A Ferrari.'

'Goodness,' she breathed, eyes widening. 'I'm impressed—so will Tom be! Ferraris are racing cars, aren't they?'

'They race a version of this one,' he agreed. 'Who's looking after your son while you're away?'

'Tom doesn't need any looking after; I've brought him up to look after himself. He can wash and iron his own clothes, cook, tidy his room—he's very self-sufficient. But his older sister is there too; she's nineteen.'

'What's her name?'

'Vicky—short for Victoria.'

'Does she look like you?'

Bianca's mouth curved into a tender, reminiscent smile. 'No, she takes after her father—she has his colouring; Rob was fair, and Vicky has blonde hair and hazel eyes, like his. She's like him in character, too. Rob was very level-tempered, a large, fair man with a calm personality.' Talking about Rob reminded her of their happy years together; she missed him so much... She gave a deep sigh.

Another car shot past them and Gil had to brake without warning to avoid crashing into the back of it. He muttered what sounded like furious swear words in Spanish and sounded his horn furiously, glaring after the other car.

After that he didn't say anything at all, staring straight ahead with a dark frown on his face until they reached the hotel. He parked outside the main entrance, and insisted on walking her to her suite.

A security man was walking past; he saluted Gil who nodded to him and spoke to him in Spanish. The man, dark and swarthy, in his thirties, heavily built and wearing a dark uniform, gave Bianca a quick, searching look, then looked back at Gil and nodded, answering him in Spanish. Clearly they were talking about her, and Bianca wished she spoke their language.

She walked into the building and up the stairs to her apartment. Just before she got there Gil caught up with her. 'What was all that about?' she asked him.

'I was telling him to be especially watchful around your apartment.' He gave her a wry look. 'Now don't start getting agitated about that; it was just a sensible precaution.'

Her nerves had tightened up again. 'I thought nobody could get in here!'

'Our security is very tight. There's a man on the gates, and the perimeter walls are electrified. The grounds are patrolled day and night. If anyone did get through our net how would he know where to find you, anyway? He would have to wander around, or hang about, looking for you, and that would make him very conspicuous. So you have nothing to worry about.'

'Oh, don't I?' she grimaced, getting out her key to unlock the front door. 'I'm beginning to think I should go back home. This isn't going to be much of a holiday, holed up in my apartment as if I were the criminal instead of the guy who attacked me!'

'I'll make sure you see something of our region,' Gil promised, following her into the apartment. The shutters were closed over the windows and the room was dark and shadowy.

She knocked into a chair on her way to the window, and stopped dead. Gil almost cannoned into her. Her pulses went into overdrive.

'I—I'll p-put the light on,' she stammered, moving to search for the light switch, but she had been here such a short time that she couldn't remember where it was situated. Agitated, she fumbled along the wall, tripped

over something that she realised a second too late was
Gil's foot, and stumbled stupidly into him, her face
hitting his chest. Suddenly breathless, she was too taken
aback to move away for a minute. She could hear a
strange, distant thumping and thought it was her heart
until it came closer and she realised it was Gil's heart
beating right below her cheek.

His hand curled round her throat, under her chin,
pushing her head backwards. Her eyes were growing accustomed to the dark; she looked up at him dazedly,
seeing his face as a pale oval glimmering above her. It
came closer; she could see the brightness of his grey eyes,
the black circle of his pupil in the centre. In the dark,
it was like looking at a bird of prey, a hunting hawk.

'Why are you so nervous?' he murmured, and she
watched his mouth move, her knees giving way.

'I...' Her voice died in her throat as she swallowed
convulsively.

'What's wrong, Bianca?' he asked softly, his mouth
coming down closer, then closer still.

'Oh,' she said wildly. 'Oh, no...'

'No, what?' Gil asked against her parted mouth, and
she groaned.

His tongue-tip slid along her lower lip and she moaned
again. 'I—I mustn't,' she stammered.

'Why not?' he asked, his tongue moving right inside
her mouth as he spoke, and she trembled, clutching him
to stop herself falling to pieces because the pleasure of
tasting his mouth was so intense it was like dying; a
piercing excitement had begun inside her, a bewildering
mix of pain and delight.

'Gil...no...'

'Shh...' he murmured, his voice husky, and then he
was kissing her hotly and she shut her eyes, let her body

yield to the pressure of his hand against her back, drawing her closer. This was what she had wanted from the first instant she saw him, almost naked in the sunlight, his beautiful body glittering with drops of water, his skin golden and smooth, his body riveting. As she remembered how he had looked that first morning, desire ran through her like a flame and she shuddered in his arms, kissing him back, her mouth meeting the insistent pressure of his with equal hunger.

She ran her hands up his chest, the warmth of his skin coming through his shirt and permeating her palms. The body under his shirt was firm and muscled; she felt her way upwards, slowly, touched his strong neck, felt the hot beat of his pulse under her fingertips. His blood ran there; she felt the race of excitement in his veins and an answering race in her own.

He wants me, she thought, shivering, and God knows I want him. I have ever since I first saw him. She knew that this could have happened then, that very first moment; her desire had been a primitive impulse over which her mind had no control; she had felt it beat up inside her as she'd looked at him, and if anything it was stronger now, more powerful.

The physical need of the past empty three years had grown into a force as devastating as a tidal wave. It was crashing now against the last frail restraints she had built up against it. She shuddered with the impact of that force.

Gil groaned, slowly ran his hand down from her throat and caressed her full, warm breasts. A deep gasp of pleasure broke from her, and then the hand behind her slid up inside her T-shirt and undid her bra. A second later she felt his hands cupping her naked breasts. His lips slid from her mouth to her neck, where his teeth grazed her; he opened his mouth on her flesh and her head fell back; she couldn't stop groaning, shaking; she was so hot, she was on fire.

Suddenly he lifted her off the floor, half over his shoulder; he began walking with her. She was in a sensual trance, knowing what was going to happen and wanting it so much that she couldn't make herself stop him. Why should she stop him? Why shouldn't she take what she wanted, and to hell with the consequences?

He carried her into the shadowy bedroom and threw back the bedcover; he pulled off her sandals, laid her on the cool linen sheet; she heard him tearing off his clothes, dropping them on the floor as he had her sandals.

Hot and cold, flushed and shivering, Bianca tried to think, tried to make herself break out of her daze.

If Rob could see me he'd be so disgusted, she thought with a sudden sick pang. Am I really going to go to bed with a man I hardly know? I haven't even known him a week yet. Some women may go in for quick holiday romances, leaping into bed without a second thought, but I'm not like that. Rob would despise me if he knew.

She sat up, white and sick, and tried to slide off the bed, but Gil was in her way, and he was naked now.

She froze, heart beating hard and fast, breathless and shaking. She couldn't take her eyes off him; her mouth went dry.

He looked down at her; she felt his eyes piercing her, reading the hunger she couldn't hide.

'May I take your clothes off, or would you rather do it yourself?' he whispered.

She sat there, all eyes. She couldn't get a word out and couldn't move, only stare at him, a deep, burning ache inside her, between her thighs.

He knelt on the bed and reached for her, and her nerves jumped.

'No!' she said, stiffening. 'I can't, Gil. Rob would hate me...'

His eyes flashed like lightning in the darkness of the room. 'He's dead. You aren't. How much longer are you going to wait? What are you expecting—permission from the grave?'

She winced. 'Don't!'

He said more gently, 'Three years is long enough, Bianca. You're alive; you have a right to a full and meaningful life, a right to love and be loved, not exist in some half-life, like a nun in a convent. Rob couldn't blame you for that—or was he petty and mean-minded?'

'Rob was generous, a kind man, warm-hearted and loving!'

'Then why would he want you to be unhappy for the rest of your life?' Gil asked, and then he reached for her again and drew her T-shirt over her head.

He undressed her slowly and she no longer protested or tried to stop him. She felt his pleasure as he took her clothes off, was weak with her own pleasure at having his hands gently touch her, each movement as much an act of love as the act itself could be, a sensual ritual, her clothes discarded item by item until she was as naked as he was.

It was three years since a man had seen her totally naked, and she felt very self-conscious, exposed and defenceless.

He sat down on the bed beside her and looked at her—the room was full of a breathing, thick silence, and her eyes darkened under his stare.

Was this how she had been looking at him? Had he felt the way she felt now?

He leaned his face against her bare breasts, groaning, his lips pressed against her flesh.

'I want you so much I feel sick.'

She quivered in response, sighing at the intimacy of having his mouth move there, over the satiny, cool skin. She reached for his hair, stroked it, then her eyes closed, and she rested her face on the top of his head.

'I've never felt this way before,' Gil whispered. 'The first time I saw you, standing on your balcony looking down at me, my stomach seemed to drop out of me.'

A little gasp broke out of her. 'That's how I felt.' It was a relief to say it aloud, to admit how she had felt that first day.

'I've got to have you,' he said in a thickened voice. 'Bianca, let me make love to you—I've been thinking about nothing else since we first met; it's driving me out of my mind.'

He lifted his head and she saw his eyes, volcanic with desire; his face was tense, jaw clenched.

What did he see? she wondered, staring back at him and feeling the same urgent, driving need she saw in him.

She didn't know which of them moved first, but suddenly they were kissing with such passion that she almost fainted. Trembling, she fell backwards on the bed, and he came with her, on top of her, his body moving between her opening thighs as if they had done this a thousand times before. The weight of him was so familiar, so right; she put her arms around him and held him close, her legs going round him too, enfolding him.

Suddenly she remembered the morning of her fortieth birthday, her dream just before waking up, the dream where Rob had turned into a faceless stranger while they were making love.

Here it was again, but this time she was wide awake, it was no dream, and the stranger had a face.

Was that what she had been telling herself in her dream? That however much she mourned Rob the truth was that she was alive, and she still needed love—she was a woman with unfulfilled needs and had to stop living in the past? The man without a face had been a symbol more than a real man; the fact that he was a stranger had been the important thing about him—her unconscious had been telling her that she had to find someone else; she needed the fulfilment of sex as much as she needed air and food and sunshine.

She had not wanted to admit that, was still nervous of admitting it now—but it was true, wasn't it? This desire burning deep inside her for a man she hardly knew was not mere lust, it was a need for love, a very basic human need.

'What's wrong? Don't turn off me again,' Gil muttered, his face burrowing between her breasts. 'Don't think about him, damn you! Don't you know how jealous that makes me? Every time you say his name I feel as if you've stabbed me.'

She lay still, horrified. 'Gil!' The admission shocked her; it hadn't occurred to her that he might be jealous of her dead husband. She bit her lip. She had been so busy thinking about her own feelings, her own problems, that she hadn't once tried to look at the situation through Gil's eyes.

He lifted his head again to look at her, a faintly sulky look on his face. 'What do you expect? You keep telling me how much you loved him and how much you miss him. I understand—I try to, anyway. But I want you to love me. I certainly don't want you thinking about him when you're with me.'

Anguished, she said, 'Rob was part of my life, part of me, for twenty years, Gil. How can I forget him altogether? I feel guilty anyway because I'm here, with you, in bed.'

'I know you do. You keep saying so.' He was getting angry, his face fierce. 'Just put him out of your head, Bianca. I want you all to myself; I'm not sharing you. I'm not making love to you while you think of him.'

'I wouldn't! I... That's a terrible thing to say!' She pushed at his shoulders, getting angry herself. 'I don't think this is a good idea; I shouldn't be doing this. It's a mistake. I think you should go.'

He stared down at her, his eyes glittering in the shadows. His voice deepened, became dark and husky. 'I could make you want me; I could make you forget him.'

'Not in this mood,' she threw back at him. 'You're too angry. I wouldn't enjoy making love to you when you're like this. I'm sorry if it makes you jealous to know I loved my husband, but I'm not going to pretend I never think of him any more. I can't erase him from my life. He's still part of it, in my children, in my memories. I wouldn't ask you to forget you ever met your wife.'

'I wish I could,' he said curtly. 'It isn't the same! You loved your husband. Mady was a mistake—she took me in completely, but once the illusion wore off and I saw the truth I walked away without a backward glance. I certainly would never think of her when I was with you. The two of you couldn't be less alike.'

Then he swung off the bed and began to pull on his clothes. Bianca sat on the edge of the bed and did the same; she had just pushed her feet into her sandals when Gil strode out of the bedroom and into the living-room to throw open the shutters. The late afternoon sun flooded in, and she winced at the illumination of the scene: the dishevelled bed, the indentation in the pillows where their heads had lain.

While she was out the maids had been in and cleaned the whole apartment; if it weren't for the disorder of the bed, you would hardly have known anyone was using the place, except that her clothes hung in the wardrobes and were folded in a chest of drawers, her nightdress was draped across the end of the bed, as the maid always left it, and there was a little pile of books and English women's magazines on the bedside table.

Gil walked back towards her, his face taut and pale. 'Let me know if you ever decide to rejoin the land of the living!' he muttered.

She bent her head and stared at the white rug beside the bed, not bothering to answer.

After a tense little silence he picked up the top book on her bedside table, the latest detective story by one of Bianca's favourite writers.

'Have you read this?'

'Not yet, I only began it yesterday, but so far it's very good.'

'I read it last week—it's terrific; I couldn't put it down.' His long fingers flicked through the pages, then he closed the book and looked at the titles of the other books, which were all novels. 'Do you read much?'

A bubble of hysteria formed in her throat. The exchange was so stilted, a polite conversation between two strangers—but then that was what they were, wasn't it? Strangers...who had somehow got into this very intimate, personal situation far too fast, and now did not know what to say to each other.

'I don't get much time for reading,' she said in the same stiff, unreal voice. 'Except in bed, late at night, when I'm usually too tired to read for long.'

His grey eyes flicked at her, glittering. 'Sleeping alone isn't good for you. A book is no substitute for a man.'

Her face turned scarlet. She gave him a furious look, stood up, and walked out of the bedroom, towards the door of her apartment. Gil followed her coolly. She opened the door and stood back to let him pass her.

'Goodbye, Señor Marquez!'

He gave her a look that made her ears boom with hypertension, but he said nothing, just walked out. Bianca slammed the door after him.

CHAPTER SIX

BIANCA needed some air, she was so hot, and it would be nice to feel cool water on her overheated skin. After hurriedly changing into a black and white striped swimsuit, she went out to the swimming-pool below her balcony, where she had first seen Gil, and lowered herself gratefully into the water. Most of the hotel guests were down at the beach, she realised, hearing loud voices, laughter and music from that direction. There was nobody else in the pool; she had it to herself.

She swam a few lengths energetically, then slowed down. The sun was low on the horizon, the air full of the sound of bird-calls and the flapping of wings as they flew between the trees. The garden of the hotel was almost tropical, full of palms and wide-leaved trees swathed in creepers, some of them vivid with blue, red and purple flowers. Bianca floated on her back, staring up at the deepening blue of the sky—she would have to go in soon but she was reluctant to move yet; she felt physically content, euphoric after her exercise.

Voices near by startled her. Lifting her head, she looked around. Freddie was walking past with her husband and children, after hours on the beach, from the look of them, all wearing swimsuits, carrying towels and books, sunglasses pushed up into their hair, their faces sun-flushed, their bodies sandy. After saying hello, Karl and the children ran on to their apartment to have showers while Freddie paused to chat to Bianca, who had swum to the end of the pool and was treading water, her wet hair plastered to her head.

'It's been a lovely day here,' Freddie told her. 'We were on the beach most of the day! How did you enjoy Granada? Isn't the Alhambra sensational?'

'Fabulous,' agreed Bianca, wondering how Freddie knew where she had been. Had Gil told her? Did Freddie know that Gil had followed her to Granada? Bianca didn't like to ask; she didn't want to discuss Gil with his sister-in-law; she didn't want to admit a personal interest in him. Instead, she talked about the Alhambra—the palace and the amazing Generalife, the gardens surrounding it, their shady walks, the wonderful fountains of roses, the clove scent of carnations scenting the air, the dazzling colours and perfumes assaulting the senses.

'I love it too,' agreed Freddie. 'But it's always so crowded with people. I'd love to go there when it was shut to the public...but then, I suppose, I am the public, so it would be shut to me too!'

Bianca laughed. 'That's just what I thought, and Gil said that tourism kills the thing it loves, which is so true! The more of us that travel, the more impossible it gets to enjoy the places we go to see! But all the same, while I'm here, I would like to see any other interesting places there are around here—can you recommend any?'

'You ought to go to Ronda—it's one of the oldest cities in Spain, not too far to drive from here; I'm sure there are coaches that go there. It's up in the hills, the most amazing place—it's cut in half by a huge gorge with a bridge over it; you can lean over and look down about fifty feet, all these great jagged rocks and trees and creepers growing out of them. It gives me vertigo. Half the town is modern Spanish, with long, straight streets, and on the other side of the gorge there's the old Moorish

town, which is all alleys and windy little streets, with a
palace they call Casa del Rey Moro...the palace of the
Moorish king...and there's a cathedral that used to be
the mosque. Bullfighting was started in Ronda by some
famous bullfighter called Pedro Romera, right back in
the eighteenth century; they're very proud of that there.
At one time the hills around the town—the Serrania de
Ronda—were full of some pretty bloodthirsty bandits.
I think these days most of them are working in restaurants and hotels, judging by the prices of drinks
around the bar down on the beach!'

'It's the same in tourist spots all over the world these
days, isn't it?' said Bianca.

'I suppose so. It cost me a fortune to have dinner in
London a few months back! Talking of dinner, Karl and
I wondered if you would have dinner with us in the hotel
dining-room tomorrow? And don't worry...the children
are going to eat in the apartment.'

'Oh—oh, thank you, that's very kind,' stammered
Bianca, wondering if Gil was going to make up a
foursome with them, afraid of seeing him again. It would
be too embarrassing, remembering what had happened
in her apartment earlier. She wouldn't be able to look
at him!

But she didn't want to hurt Freddie's feelings, either,
which left her in an impasse. What was she to do? She
liked Freddie very much and Karl seemed pleasant. She
would enjoy dinner with them in other circumstances—
it was just a pity they were related to Gil Marquez.

'So you'll come?' pressed Freddie, watching her
curiously.

How could she refuse? She could hardly plead
another engagement.

'I'd love to,' she said huskily, very flushed; she looked at Freddie and away, restlessly, her heart beating far too fast. 'What time?'

'About eight? You remember how late the Spanish eat? Can you meet us in the piano bar for drinks at eight?'

Bianca nodded. 'Eight in the piano bar. OK.'

Freddie turned away then stopped and looked back over her shoulder. 'Oh...I forgot to say...they're having a band in after dinner, for dancing; they do that several times a week and it's fun—I love to dance, don't you? So wear something you can dance in.'

Bianca looked at her uncertainly. 'Well...actually I wanted to go into Marbella to buy a dress I spotted in a shop window... The trouble is, I'm not supposed to leave the hotel grounds; Gil insists I have someone with me if I do.'

'Well, why don't you come with us to Marbella tomorrow? We were going shopping there anyway; the children have been begging to go to town, to buy presents to take back to their friends, and Karl and I have family presents to buy. We have our car with us; we drove down here from Germany. We could fly and hire a car, of course, but Karl likes to have his own car with him; it's a Mercedes—we know we can rely on it and it has plenty of room in it for the luggage. It's very spacious; Karl and the kids can sit in the back and you can sit in the front with me.'

'Are you sure?' said Bianca.

'Absolutely sure. We'd love to take you, and I'll come along and help you buy the dress; I know your Spanish isn't very good.'

'You're very kind; thank you very much.'

'Not at all. Why not have breakfast with us? Eight o'clock—is that OK for you? We'll go after that, shall we, at about nine? The earlier we go the better—the shops won't be so crowded at about ten, but the rush-hour will be over as far as traffic is concerned.'

'OK.' Bianca nodded and Freddie smiled at her, then hurried away.

Hauling herself out of the pool, Bianca picked up her towelling robe and put it on, towelled her hair and dried her feet before pushing them into her sandals, then she walked back to her apartment, passing the security man to whom Gil had spoken much earlier. He gave her a sharp look and nodded politely.

Back in her apartment she showered, ate a very light supper—salad and a little fruit—then read for an hour or two before she went to bed. She must have been immensely tired, because she slept like a log, and if she dreamt she didn't remember it in the morning. She woke up when her alarm went off at seven-thirty; the bedroom was full of pale primrose light, and outside she heard the birds singing in the trees. For a moment she was so drowsy and disorientated that she couldn't remember where she was or what had woken her up, then she realised her alarm was buzzing and she hurriedly leaned over to turn it off.

Swinging her legs out of the bed, she stood up, stretching, gave a convulsive yawn then hurried off to the bathroom. It didn't take her long to get ready and walk over to the hotel for breakfast.

She found Freddie and her family there already, Karl eating cheese and thin slices of German sausage, the children eating fruit and yoghurt, Freddie toying with a slice of toast and a cup of black coffee. They waved and told her to join them—there was a free chair for her.

'Did you sleep?'

'Too well. I couldn't wake up.' Bianca yawned, hurriedly covering her mouth. 'Sorry; I can't seem to stop.'

Freddie yawned too. 'Don't worry, I feel the same way. The funny thing is, I slept very well.'

'Same here; odd, isn't it? Oh, well, I'd better get something to eat.' Bianca went off to the buffet table to collect some orange juice and some green figs, over which she poured a little natural, plain yoghurt.

When she came back the children had gone and Karl and Freddie were alone, energetically discussing what to buy to take back for various relatives back in Germany.

'Your mother's very difficult to buy for,' Freddie complained. 'She hates ornaments—they need too much dusting! She never likes any clothes I choose. I can't think what to buy her.'

'Perfume?' suggested Karl.

'She only wears Dior, and she's drowning in bottles of the stuff, you should know that! You're the one who buys it for her all the time.'

He made a face. 'I can never think what to buy her. She has everything.'

'Well, lucky her!' Freddie said drily.

'How about some local lace or something made of leather?' suggested Bianca. 'That's what they're famous for in this part of Spain, isn't it?'

Freddie looked uncertainly at her husband. 'What do you think?'

'I think lace is a wonderful idea—so long as it is really high quality; Mutti is very fussy,' said Karl.

Freddie raised her brows. 'Isn't that the truth?'

Karl laughed and tweaked her ear. 'Don't be unkind about my poor little Mutti.' He stood up. 'I'll see you back at the apartment—don't be too long; we want to get to Marbella early.'

When he had gone, Freddie said drily, 'His poor little Mutti is a good five feet ten in her stockinged feet and has the muscles and punch of a boxer. The odd thing is, she is very feminine, floats around in a haze of perfume all day, and wears the most exquisite clothes. Some really good lace would be the perfect present for her; I should have thought of it myself. I have a sort of blank spot where she's concerned, that's the trouble. She terrified me when Karl first took me home to meet her, and I suppose I'm still wary of her.'

'Mother-in-laws can be a problem! Thank heavens, mine was fine.' She smiled, remembering Molly, Rob's mother, who had been kind and generous, a warm-hearted woman who adored her son. 'She's dead now, though. I was glad about that when Rob died—it would have been such a blow to her; she adored him—he was her only son.'

'Gil is an only son, and he was terribly spoilt,' said Freddie.

Bianca nodded, instantly self-conscious, aware of an immediate flush in her face and trying to hide it by taking a sip of her coffee. Why did his name always come up when they talked? Did Freddie think she was obsessed with him?

Of course not. He's her brother-in-law and she knows I know him! she argued with herself. It's perfectly natural for her to mention him from time to time. Stop being so hypersensitive.

'What about you?'

'Me?' Bianca was confused, too busy thinking about Gil to work out what Freddie meant.

'Are you an only child?'

Bianca shook her head. 'No, I have a brother, Jon; there were just the two of us, though, and my mother spoilt him—she thought the sun shone out of Jon. She was one of those mothers who prefer their sons to their daughters—she would have loved to have lots of sons. She couldn't have any more after she had me, so she poured all her love into Jon. I don't think he has ever really grown up because of that, actually—he expects every woman he meets to dote on him the way Mum did, and of course they don't—they want a grown-up man, not a Peter Pan. That's why I made certain that my own son, Tom, could take care of himself. I taught him to do his own washing and ironing, to make his bed, and cook, just the same as his sister. I don't want Tom growing up as useless as his uncle Jon.'

Freddie nodded. 'I couldn't agree more. What does your mother think of the way you're bringing up your boy? Does she keep a critical eye on you? My mother-in-law does; she's always telling me where I'm going wrong in the way I treat my children.'

'My mother's dead, I'm afraid.'

'Oh, I'm sorry.' Freddie gave her an uncertain look, eyes apologetic.

'It was some years ago—she died not long after my husband, actually.'

Freddie's face was full of warm sympathy. 'That must have been a great shock to you—to have to bear two deaths so close together.'

Bianca sighed. 'It takes a long time to get over it. For a while I felt death was haunting me. My father died a few months after my mother.'

'Oh, poor Bianca!'

'He was in his seventies, and really still very active, but I think he had lost the will to live. He missed my mother so much; they had been married for over forty years, had become almost one person; he was like someone who has lost half of himself. He was never the same man after she died; he wouldn't go out, wouldn't come to live with me, although I begged him to, he never seemed to eat much, and in the end he died in his sleep— a heart attack, the doctor told me, and I am sure that was what it was; his heart just gave up beating.'

'How wonderful that they were so happy together, though. You hear so many horror stories about marriages that don't work—it's good to hear about one that did.'

'Yes,' said Bianca, a smile in her eyes. 'It was a very happy marriage. So was mine, and I can see your marriage is a happy one, too.'

Freddie's face lit up, her mouth curving happily. 'Yes, we've been very lucky; we have a lovely home and terrific children—and we are very happy together.' She looked at her watch. 'It's getting late. I'd better go and get ready. Can you meet us outside the hotel in...' she looked at the remains of Bianca's breakfast, her half-drunk cup of coffee '...say, twenty minutes?'

Bianca nodded. 'I'll be there.'

She finished her coffee while Freddie was hurrying away, and a few minutes later made her way to her apartment to put on make-up, brush her hair, collect a shopping bag. In good time she went back to the main hotel building but there was no sign as yet of Freddie and her family. Bianca wandered along a path, admiring a display of blue, purple and yellow pansies under some slender young silver birch trees.

'What are you up to?'

The voice made her jump; she swung round, her pulses leaping under her skin, and looked up at Gil, knowing her colour was high and her eyes feverish.

He looked into her eyes, a half-smile curling his mouth, intimacy and warmth in his gaze.

'Oh... hello,' she said, looking away again hurriedly. Oh, stop it! she told herself, but she couldn't get over the way he looked—those striking good looks were intensified by the clothes he was wearing today—the hotelier's uniform of dark suit and white shirt, discreet dark red tie. 'You must get very hot in those clothes!' she said huskily and he laughed.

'Later in the year it becomes unbearable to wear them, but guests expect the hotel manager to dress suitably,' he said wryly. There was a pause, and she felt his gaze wandering down over her, from her dark head to her sandalled feet. 'Talking of clothes, why are you wearing that very elegant dress? Not that I don't love the way it looks on you—it's just the colour of these flowers, isn't it? A wonderful dark, velvety blue. It suits you. But it isn't exactly the thing to wear on the beach. It would be ruined in half an hour. I hope you weren't planning to go anywhere? You know you can't leave the hotel grounds without protection, not while those two little thugs are free.'

'I'm going shopping in Marbella——' she began, and he curtly interrupted.

'Oh, no, you're not!' He sounded really furious and she looked up at him defiantly.

'With your sister-in-law,' she finished, her voice rising over his.

He stared, his brows jerking together. 'Freddie?'

She nodded. 'And Karl, and the children. They should be here any minute, to drive me into town.'

'Why on earth do you want to go into town? You should be down on the beach on a lovely day like this—not wandering around the streets of Marbella.'

'I have some shopping to do, and, anyway, I liked what I saw of Marbella the first night I got here; I want to see it in daylight.'

'If you'd told me, I'd have taken you!'

She gave him a quick look, even more flushed, then looked down again. 'You're working.'

'I can arrange for someone to take over from me.'

She didn't have to answer that because a large white Mercedes swept towards them and Gil shot a glance at it, muttering, 'That's Karl now.' He caught hold of her arm, his cool fingers possessive. 'Be careful, Bianca. Do you hear me? Keep your wits about you while you're out. I don't want to be told you've been mown down by a motorbike in Marbella.'

She nodded, quivering at his touch. 'I'll be careful. I must go—Freddie and Karl are waving.'

'Damn Freddie and Karl!' he said through his teeth. 'Bianca, I don't like you going out alone...'

'I won't be alone!'

'Without me,' he said roughly, and her breath caught.

'I'm sure I'll be fine with Freddie and Karl,' she said huskily, pulling free. Without a backward look she hurried off towards the white Mercedes.

Karl and the children were in the back of the car, Freddie was behind the wheel. Leaning over, Freddie opened the front passenger seat and gestured; Bianca climbed in beside her and as she did so Gil arrived, closed the door on her and leaned on the half-open window, looking into the car.

'If anything happens to her while she's out with you two I'll kill the pair of you!' he grimly told his sister-in-law and her husband.

'We'll look after her, don't worry,' Karl said from the back of the car, his voice calmly reassuring.

'We won't leave her alone for a second,' Freddie promised.

Bianca shot Gil a glance and met his grey eyes; they glittered darkly at her, the black pupils so large, they were all she could see.

'Be careful!' he warned fiercely.

She nodded and he withdrew from the window. Freddie drove off with a squeal of tyres on gravel and a moment later they were out on the road to Marbella in the early morning traffic and Bianca was able to relax with a faint sigh, smothered before her companions could hear it and draw their own conclusions, which might be rather too accurate, she felt.

They spent a very enjoyable couple of hours in Marbella. After they had parked and walked into the old town, Karl and the children went off on some expedition of their own while Freddie and Bianca went in search of the dress shop in whose window Bianca had seen the flamenco-style dress.

'I do hope it hasn't been sold! It was probably a one-off, and I really loved it.'

She was on edge as they walked, constantly looking around, half expecting to see a leather-clad figure on a motorbike, jumping at every sound...the bang of a door, a car starting, a dog barking.

When they reached the narrow little street they were looking for it was worse. Bianca felt her nerves prickle as she caught sight of the tapas bar outside which she had been attacked just a few nights ago. So much had happened since. It seemed like weeks, not days ago, yet coming back made it all come sharply into focus, raw and immediate, and very painful, as if it had only happened last night.

'Is that the shop?' asked Freddie when she stopped walking and froze on the narrow pavement in more or less the same spot on which it had taken place.

Bianca pulled herself together, forced a smile. 'Yes,' she said, then she looked at the window display and her eyes lit up. 'Yes! That's the shop, and that's the dress! It's still there.'

'Hey, that is gorgeous!' Freddie said, eyes widening as she stared at the dress. 'And very Spanish! I couldn't wear it, but I can see it will suit you perfectly, Bianca; you have the right colouring and the right figure for it.'

'Do you really think so?'

In broad daylight, the dress was even more boldly dramatic, the red the colour of blood, the neckline lower than anything she had worn for years, the waist tight, the skirt full and cascading with frills of black lace. It was not a dress for anyone timid or retiring, and Bianca didn't know if she had the nerve to carry it off in public.

She considered it uncertainly, but Freddie was enthusiastic. 'Go on, go in and try it on! What have you got to lose? I'll tell you if it doesn't look good on you, I promise.' She took hold of Bianca's wrist and dragged her into the shop where a large, statuesque Spanish lady in a black dress with a white lace collar took charge of Bianca and, having been told it was the dress in the window which interested her, carried her and the dress off to a fitting-room.

Bianca, by then, was half hoping the dress would not be her size, but it was; what was more, it fitted her like a glove.

The Spanish manageress burbled in Spanish at her while Bianca stared dumbfounded at her own reflection, thrown back to her from all sides. Every wall in the little room held a full-length mirror. She was transformed the red dress gave her a style and passion that alarmed her, the cascading frills and glimpses of her legs as disturbing as the neckline which left so much of her white breasts bare.

'On you, is lovely,' the Spanish woman managed, beaming over her shoulder, tweaking the neckline even lower.

Bianca tweaked it right back up again. She was not going around half naked.

Undeterred, the other woman cooed at her. 'Very Spanish, for the dance, flamenco... you English? You look Spanish in this.'

Freddie knocked on the door of the fitting-room. 'Can I come in?'

'Yes,' said Bianca reluctantly, and in the mirrored walls saw Freddie standing staring in the doorway, eyes round and saucer-shaped, mouth open too.

When she had her breath back Freddie said, 'How much is it?'

Bianca told her.

'Buy it,' said Freddie. 'It's a bargain. You look a million dollars, and it's a classic; you'll be able to wear it for years and years, so long as you stay the same size.'

After a brief hesitation Bianca had to admit that she wanted the dress; it looked even better than she had dared dream. She paid for it and the manageress packed it up in tissue paper and a large cardboard box, then Bianca and Freddie walked back through the narrow, windy little streets of Marbella, buying fruit and vegetables from a stall at a local market, and then some locally made goat's cheese, rolled in chopped pepper, some crusty, golden bread and a bag of Churros, cooked right in front them on a small gas ring—they turned out to be long, twisty,

freshly cooked doughnuts, smothered in sugar while they
were still hot.

Eventually they found Karl and the children sitting in
a café in a flower-decked square, drinking hot chocolate, and sat down with them. The two boys and their
sister were excitedly full of what they had bought to take
back as presents for friends and relatives, and when they
asked what Bianca had bought she only had to say, 'A
dress!' for them to lose interest.

The sun was getting quite hot; the shade of the café
blind was pleasant, the hot chocolate delicious. They sat
there for a long time, lazily staring around at the passers-
by and the narrow streets, the old buildings, the distant
blue haze of the mountains which could be seen from
where they sat.

A sound made Bianca stiffen. A motorbike was
weaving its way around the square; she saw the domed
helmets of the rider and his passenger, the black leather,
and she went white, holding her breath.

'What's wrong?' Freddie asked, staring at her.

The motorbike shot past them and disappeared up a
side-street. Bianca sagged in relief.

'Nothing,' she said shakily. 'Nothing at all. Maybe we
should be getting back to the hotel, though?'

They got back to the hotel just in time for lunch and
met up again in the dining room. The usual buffet was
laid out—Bianca collected salad, great pink prawns
cooked with rice and peas, a slice of cold chicken and
some coleslaw. Karl had ordered white wine and insisted
that she must have some.

She sipped it, listening to him talking about the head-
lines in that day's papers; Karl had strong views on in-
ternational politics. He was obviously a clever man,
strong-minded and forceful. Bianca was struck, too, by

the way he and Freddie talked to each other and to their children. The warmth between them all made her envious, nostalgic, a little lonely—it reminded her of the happiness she had had with Rob, all gone now, vanished like summer flowers when the frosts of winter started.

She felt shut out of the circle of family which bound the others together. She ached for the days that had gone. She missed her children. She hadn't rung them since she arrived—she would ring them tonight, she decided, when they were both likely to be at home.

She spent the afternoon on the beach, swimming, sunbathing, resting under a striped umbrella and occasionally having the beach attendant bring her a glass of sparkling mineral water stiff with chunks of ice and slices of lemon. Freddie and her family were near by, Karl and the children playing energetic beach games as usual while Freddie watched them indulgently without stirring herself from her mattress.

When the sun began to slide down the sky, and the air chilled, Bianca went back to her apartment, had a leisurely bath and then put on a robe and sat on her bed, painting her nails while she watched a Spanish version of an American film she had seen several times. She couldn't understand a word that was spoken but she knew, at least, what was happening!

At half-past six, when she could reasonably hope that her children were both likely to be in, she rang home, but it was neither of them who picked up the phone. Instead, she heard a voice she recognised at once with a leap of alarm.

'Judy? Judy, what are you doing there? Is something wrong? Has something happened to one of the children? What——?'

'Calm down!' Judy said, laughing. 'Typical of you Bianca, to get into a panic over nothing. There's nothing wrong with your precious kids. I called round to check that they were OK, that's all, and to bring them a hot meal. We had a blizzard yesterday and snow blocked all the roads; it's so cold I'm wearing two sweaters! I was worried about Vicky and Tom coping if the pipes froze while they were out all day with the central heating turned off so I popped in on my way home from the shop. They're fine. They left the heating on, it seems! A bit extravagant, but in the circumstances a smart move because the house was very warm when I arrived. I brought them a lamb casserole I'd cooked overnight—they only have to reheat it and it's full of vegetables, so they won't have to cook anything to go with it. I put it in the oven for them.'

Touched, Bianca said, 'You are kind! That was very thoughtful; I'm grateful, Judy. I hope they said thank you.'

'Several times, with real feeling—when I arrived they were squabbling over whose turn it was to cook the baked beans on toast!'

Stricken, Bianca groaned. 'Is that all they're eating?'

Judy laughed. 'Of course not! If it wasn't so cold they would be living on no-cook salad and yoghurt, I gathered, but Tom was starving because it was so cold and he wanted a hot meal. Don't you worry—they are getting enough to eat. You aren't to feel guilty—I know you! The fridge was full of food, and Tom had a huge bagful of apples he was grazing on when I arrived. So, how is the holiday going?'

'Fine,' Bianca said a little self-consciously.

'Met any tall, dark, handsome strangers yet?'

'Well...' Bianca's voice trailed off; she bit her lip. She had not had an answer prepared; she had not been expecting to talk to Judy. She had been caught off guard. Neither of her children would have asked her such a question.

'You have!' crowed Judy. 'Well, come on... tell me all!'

'There's nothing to tell.'

'What's his name?'

Bianca suddenly wanted to confide in someone; she needed to talk about him, about the way she felt, and Judy knew her better than anyone else in the world now.

'Gil,' she said. 'Gil Marquez.'

'Funny name,' Judy said frankly. 'It sounds...'

'Spanish—he is! He's the manager of this hotel. Oh, Judy, he's unbelievable... you should see him on the beach; his skin is like gold silk...'

'Does it feel like it too?'

Bianca took a deep breath, then whispered, 'Yes, just like silk.'

Judy gasped audibly. 'Bianca... you haven't... You have, haven't you? God, that was quick work; you've only been there a few days! I'd never have believed it— you of all people!'

Crimson, Bianca hurriedly protested. 'I didn't mean... We haven't been to... I mean for heaven's sake, Judy, of course we haven't.'

'You haven't been to bed with him?' Judy asked bluntly.

'No, certainly not!'

'So how do you know how his skin feels?'

'Judy! I've seen a lot of him since I arrived, OK?'

Judy giggled. 'You must have done! On the beach, did you say? Or has the action moved up into your bedroom?'

'You have a dreadful mind!' Bianca told her crossly.

'And you didn't answer the question. Never mind, I think I get the picture. I'm glad you're having a good time—this was just what you needed—but just remember that holiday romances always fizzle out when you get back home, so keep your head, and for God's sake don't sleep with him without a condom, however gorgeous he is!'

'I didn't say I... I wouldn't... There's no question of...' Bianca was completely at a loss, spluttering and very flushed. She heard Judy laughing again.

'OK, don't go to pieces. Anyway, what's the weather like there?'

That was a safer subject; Bianca relaxed a little. 'It's been wonderful, quite hot today, in fact. Hot enough to sit on the beach all afternoon, and swim in the sea. I'm getting a tan.'

Judy groaned. 'You're so lucky! Oh, here's Vicky coming in to find out who's on the phone—— It's your mum... I'll put her on now, Bianca. Have a great time and remember... be careful!'

'Judy, you won't tell them...' Bianca began, and then she heard Vicky's voice on the other end of the line.

'Mum? How's Spain?'

'Wonderful,' Bianca said quickly, and talked about the weather, the Alhambra, the hotel complex, the beach, the gardens, her apartment. She did not mention the mugging or Gil Marquez, praying that Judy wouldn't breathe a word to either Vicky or Tom.

'I've sent you postcards, from Granada and from Marbella—do you remember us going to Spain?'

'With Dad? Of course,' said Vicky oddly. 'Here's Tom, Mum—he wants to talk to you too. Bye; enjoy yourself.'

She was gone before Bianca could answer. Tom came on the line and cheerfully chattered away about his latest football match being cancelled because the pitch was frozen and covered in snow, complained about his homework and his maths teacher. Bianca felt love welling up inside her; he was so uncomplicated, so normal. He wasn't as touchy or difficult as his sister, thank heavens!

'Mum, can I have a new pair of football boots? There's this really great pair in Willows, and if I had them I just know I would get goals.'

'How much?' asked Bianca, and then, '*How much*?' in horror and disbelief when he told her. 'You have got to be kidding! I could buy myself a summer wardrobe for that much. Forget it.' Then she asked him about food. 'You aren't just living on baked beans, are you? Or was Judy exaggerating?'

'I like baked beans,' he said. 'Vicky keeps trying to make me eat her diet stuff but I'm hungry when I get home. Salad is for rabbits.'

She laughed rather helplessly. 'Try to eat protein, darling—some eggs, some cheese—nuts are good; eat lots of nuts.'

'Peanuts?' he asked suspiciously.

'Fine.'

'OK, Mum.'

She caught sight of the time and sighed. 'I've got to go, Tom; I'm going out tonight and I haven't dressed. You've got my number here, if you need me. Bye.'

It was way past seven now; she had to dress in a hurry, and when she had she was taken aback by her reflection in the mirror. She had never in her life worn a dress like this—she was stricken with uncertainty, intensely self-conscious. Who was this woman in the mirror, her black hair piled high behind her head, pinned with a great black Spanish comb, black lace floating from it? This woman in scarlet and black lace, a dress so tight that it showed every line of her body, black high-heeled shoes that gave her a height she didn't normally have—she didn't know her!

The self she was used to seeing in her mirror was a woman of forty who dressed conventionally, was sensible and responsible, worked hard, ran a home, looked after her children. Never took risks, never got excited, never wanted anything for herself, only planned for her children's future—never for a future of her own. The Bianca who had woken up on her fortieth birthday had been ground down into the ruts of her life, had had nothing to look forward to, just a quiet succession of days all the same as before, forever and ever to the edge of doom.

That was not her in the mirror. Was it? No, no, she didn't recognise that woman. Even her mouth seemed strange and unfamiliar—a disturbing scarlet bow, cushiony in the full lower lip, hot and inviting.

She gave it another startled, horrified glance. That wasn't her mouth. She picked up the black lace fan which Freddie had made her buy to go with the dress, flicked it open and lifted it to hide her mouth; over it her eyes glittered, wide and bright, with excitement, with invitation. She did not know them either.

She couldn't wear the dress to dinner tonight! She didn't have the nerve to walk into the bar to meet Freddie and Karl looking like this!

Freddie has already seen you in the dress—don't be silly! she told herself. And Karl is too preoccupied with his wife to give you a second glance.

But Gil would be there.

Oh, yes, that was what was bothering her, wasn't it? The idea of Gil seeing the feverish excitement in her eyes, in the parted redness of her mouth, in the tense curve of her body—seeing and understanding the smouldering sexual invitation in the way she looked in this intensely sexy dress. She didn't want to give him the idea that she was giving him any such message!

Don't you? she thought, looking at her reflection helplessly, fighting to calm herself. Her hands were clenched in the effort to tone down her high colour, the quiver of her mouth, the glitter of her eyes.

Who are you trying to fool? You wanted Gil the minute you saw him. You want him so much it's eating away at you night and day; you can't think of anything else!

She turned away, biting her lip. Stop it! she told herself. Shame flooded through her. What was the matter with her? Obsessed with sex, aching to have a man, at her age?

Her age? Was that it? Had waking up to find herself forty, and on the verge of middle age, thrown her entire mind and body into turmoil? Was this some sort of mid-life crisis? The next big crisis of her life would probably be when she hit the menopause and stopped being capable of having a baby—maybe this was nature's way of telling her to hurry up and grab a last chance?

Was she actually falling in love with Gil—or had her hormones simply gone crazy when it had dawned on her that time was running out? Was Gil just the first eligible man she had run into since her birthday?

It was horrifying to find yourself the prisoner of your own hormones. She felt stupid and helpless. This churning excitement, this permanent state of aroused sexuality...was it nothing but chemistry?

A brisk tap on the front door of her apartment made her jump. She swung round, her skirts flaring around her legs. A maid, come to turn down her bed?

The tap came again, louder. No, a maid would have used her pass key to come in if there was no answer.

Gil, she thought, pulses thundering, and couldn't move. It had to be Gil.

Slowly she went to the door and began to open it. Then the door was knocked wide by a body crashing into it, forcing it back right into Bianca, who was thrown across the room.

The door slammed shut. Terror paralysed her as she saw the hard, hating black eyes, the vicious face of the boy she had picked out in the police station the other day.

Her mouth opened to scream but he leapt across to her too fast for a sound to escape. His black-gloved hand rammed down on her mouth, pushing her lips back on her teeth, silencing the muffled sounds she made.

Eyes wide with terror, she fought him, trembling, trying to push him away. His thin, muscular body jerked forward, thrust itself down on her, forcing her back against the wall.

He muttered a word in Spanish; she didn't know the word but she knew he had insulted her. He looked down at her body, the full white breasts half exposed by the ruffles of black lace, the way the soft material clung to her waist and hips, fell back from her long legs.

He grinned, and Bianca felt suddenly sick. His eyes were insulting, crude, explicit. He grabbed the lace with his free hand and ripped; her breasts spilled out and he bent his head and sank his teeth into her nipple. The pain was agonising. Under his muffling hand Bianca screamed. She began to struggle wildly then, punching

him, trying to knee him in the groin as she had that
night in the Marbella street.

He was ready for her this time, though; before she
made contact he balled his fist and struck her in the face,
right between the eyes. Her head was flung violently back
and hit the wall so hard, it almost knocked her out.
Dazed and in agony, she sagged downwards, all the fight
knocked out of her.

While she was half fainting, he lifted her off the floor,
put her body over his shoulder, and carried her into the
bedroom. Bianca came back to full consciousness just
as he pushed her down on the bed.

A scream broke out of her; she tried to sit up, to get
away, but he punched her in the face again, in the mouth;
she tasted her own blood on her tongue.

He pulled a long silk scarf from round his own neck,
rammed it into her mouth, gagged her with it, caught
hold of her tumbled black hair, dragging her head painfully up off the bed, and tied the scarf in a double knot
behind her head.

Gasping and choking, Bianca tried to think—she had
to get away, she had to get away. If she were only
stronger...if she weren't so frightened. If he hits me
again I shall pass out, she thought; her face ached with
bruises, tears welled behind her lids.

The room was shadowy; the sun had gone down now
and he had not put on the electric light in here. She could
only just see his face, the lank black hair, the oily skin,
the parted, panting mouth, the glitter of his excited eyes,
the vicious intention they held.

He grabbed her dress and ripped again; the whole front
of the dress came apart, leaving her almost naked,

wearing just a bra and tiny black silk panties. His black eyes moved over her; she saw sweat on his upper lip, his tongue-tip.

'*Sí*!' he muttered, and sick terror filled her.

CHAPTER SEVEN

THE most terrifying thing about it was that Bianca blanked out; she couldn't think, wasn't even able to fight for a moment, her blue eyes stretched as wide as they could go, her breathing very rapid, each breath painful. It was as if she had known this would happen for a long time; the threat in his eyes had been there the night he'd tried to mug her in Marbella—a threat which was vicious, a desire to hurt and humiliate which had nothing to do with her at all. This was not personal—he simply hated women, all women.

He wasn't intending to rape her because he found her attractive; he didn't desire her body. He wanted to make her suffer; there was cruelty in his grin, in his black eyes, a sadistic enjoyment of her fear and helplessness. He was almost young enough to be her son and yet he made the hair stand up on her head.

He begin to unzip his trousers and the movement unfroze Bianca's brain. She went crazy, her body heaving on the bed, fighting him like a trapped animal, hoarse, muffled cries in her throat.

He drew back his arm to smash his fist into her face again, and at that second someone banged on the front door of her apartment.

The boy stiffened, was still, his head turned to listen.

Hope flooded into Bianca; someone was out there; someone might hear her. While the boy's attention was fixed on the bedroom door she managed to wrench down the scarf enough to yell.

'Help! Help!'

The boy's head swung back to her instantly; she sa
his arm move and then there was an explosion of pa
so terrible that she didn't even cry out; her head fe
back on the bed and her body went limp, sprawled c
the sheet.

For a moment all she could think about was the pa
throbbing away in her face. Blood filled her mouth wi
salty wetness. Semi-conscious, she was hardly aware
what happened next, although she heard sounds a
movements vaguely, as if from a far, far distance.

A key turned in the lock of the front door, the do
burst open and there was a stampede of feet as men can
hurtling into the apartment. The boy stumbled off t
bed and darted towards the bedroom door, either to r
out or to bolt the door, but whatever his intention
was too late. The doorway was already blocked. F
looked round wildly for a way out but two armed s
curity men grabbed him, wrenching his arms behind
back with such force that he gave a strangled cry of pa
and began to swear in Spanish. The security m
frogmarched him out of the room, ignoring his shou
and struggles.

Gil went straight to the bed, to Bianca. He winced a
went white as he looked at her bruised, swollen face, t
blood trickling from her nose. Lifting her head with gre
care and tenderness, he untied the knot in the silk sca
unwound it from around her neck, tossed the scarf
the floor.

'What did that bastard do to you? My God, I wi
I'd got to him before the men did—I'd have torn hi
limb from limb, the sadistic little swine...'

She heard his voice and tried to lift her lids; it hu
but she managed it and looked at him dazedly. She h

never in her life been so glad to see anyone; tears welled into her eyes.

'Gil.' Her voice broke. 'Oh...Gil...'

'I'm here,' he said, gently stroking the torn, tangled hair back from her face. 'I'm here, Bianca; you're safe now.'

She shuddered helplessly. 'He...' Her voice sounded thick and strange; blood was trickling from the corner of her mouth.

'Don't try to talk. Your mouth must hurt badly. You should be resting, Bianca.'

'He was going to rape me!'

'Shh...' Gil soothed her as if she were a child, patting her hair, her shoulder.

She was trembling violently, her teeth chattering like castanets. 'I'm so cold. So cold.'

'Shock,' Gil said from somewhere a long way off, and lifted her up off the bed, into his arms.

'Don't...' she cried out, panic surging back, fighting him off.

'OK, OK,' he said, and then she felt warmth surrounding her as he wrapped a quilt around her whole body, then lowered her to the bed again. 'Better?'

She shut her eyes, still shivering. 'Better,' she whispered.

'I'm going to get a doctor for you,' he said quietly. He moved away from the bed, picked up the telephone from her bedside table, and a few seconds later spoke curtly in Spanish.

After a while he put the phone down and she felt him come towards her again, sit down on the edge of her bed, feather a few strands of hair back from her temples.

'The doctor will be here soon. Bianca...' He paused; she felt him watching her, but didn't open her eyes. The shivering was slowing, warmth was percolating into her her mind was operating again, but she couldn't face Gil He had seen her like that... her hair dishevelled, he dress ripped apart, her body almost naked, her fac marked, bruised and bloody.

Gil was the last man in the world she would hav wanted to see her in that state. Shame and sickness fille her.

She shouldn't have opened the door without checkin; who was outside. There was a security window in th door, a tiny glass circle which gave you a strange view of whoever stood outside, like looking out of a goldfisl bowl. If she had looked before she'd opened the doo she would have seen him and none of it would hav happened.

If only I had... If only...

'Bianca, can you hear me? You haven't fainted, hav you?'

Reluctantly, her lids stirred.

'Bianca, the police are here; they want to see you. D you feel up to talking to them, telling them what hap pened? They want to make sure they can keep him locke up this time, so if you could make a statement at onc it would help. But if you can't face it I'll keep them away. I don't want you to feel you must, if it bother you.'

She forced her eyes open; Gil was bending over her she felt his physical presence and shrank back, chill per spiration breaking out on her skin.

'Don't...'

He frowned. 'You're not scared of me, Bianca, ar you? I'd rather cut off my right arm than hurt you— don't you know that?'

She half sobbed, half laughed. 'I'm sorry, I can't help it. Of course I know you wouldn't hurt me—of course you wouldn't.' But she didn't want him touching her or coming too close. She didn't want anyone coming too close; she needed to distance herself, to cut herself off from everyone for a while.

He sat down on the bed further away, his face pale, his brows heavy above his grey eyes. 'Do you feel up to seeing the police?'

She sighed. 'I suppose I have to?'

'Not if you don't feel you can bear it. It's up to you. When the doctor gets here he'll probably sedate you; I think maybe you should go to hospital.'

'No! I'm not seriously hurt. Just bruised.'

'You're in shock; it might be wiser if you spent a night in hospital where they can keep an eye on you.'

'I don't want to go to hospital,' she said obstinately, and then suddenly wailed, 'I want to go home!' as she was overwhelmed by a desperate yearning to be safely back in her own house, with her children.

If she had never come here this wouldn't have happened. It was a pity she had ever seen that poster in the travel agency window. She shut her eyes and remembered that day, when she'd first got the idea of a holiday in Spain—it seemed so long ago, another lifetime. So much had happened to her since she got here. It was incredible how much difference a few days could make. Time had rushed past, yet looking back she felt she had been here for months, not days. Her memories of this place were going to be crowded with incident. At home time had slowly dragged past, each day more or less the same, a gentle, tranquil, unthreatening routine of life. Why had she ever grown tired of it? Why had she wanted to get away? She didn't know when she was well off, did she?

You stupid woman! she told herself. Once you get back home there won't be any more foreign holidays, any more adventures, any more risks taken.

'How did he get in here?' she asked Gil hoarsely. 'I thought your security was supposed to be foolproof?'

'We don't know yet. The security man I warned to be extra vigilant around your apartment noticed someone vanishing into this block and knew it was not a guest, or a member of staff, so he got on the mobile phone to me to let me know, and I shot over here with a couple of other guys. I knew you should be leaving now to meet Freddie and Karl in the piano bar—I had an immediate sixth sense that something was wrong. So we came up here, and thank God we were in time.'

She felt ice trickle down her spine. 'Yes,' she whispered.

There was a tap on the door of the apartment; Gil slid off the bed and walked away, returning a moment later with a short, middle-aged man in a dark suit.

'This is Dr Perez, Bianca. I'm afraid his English isn't very good, so would you like me to stay, to translate for you?'

She shook her head. She did not want him in the room while the doctor examined her.

'Well, if you want me, I'll be in the sitting-room,' Gil said without comment, and left, closing the door behind him.

The doctor smiled at Bianca soothingly, then began a brief examination, clicking his tongue over the bruises on her face and throat. He asked her a few gentle questions; she managed to understand his limping English and he seemed to grasp her replies. She wished again that she had learnt some Spanish, and decided that before she visited any country in future she would learn at least some of their language.

He showed her a hypodermic. 'Please, sorry, I try not to hurt.'

Warily, she eyed the thing he held. 'What's in there?'

He frowned, shrugged. 'Drugs.'

'What sort of drugs?' Bianca did not much like the idea of that long needle going into her and pumping her full of unknown drugs.

The doctor sighed, making a face, then walked away, opened the door and called Gil, who came hurrying. The doctor talked fast in Spanish; Gil talked fast back to him, then came over to the bed and looked down at her, his eyes searching her bruised face.

'Well, you'll be glad to hear that the doctor doesn't think you need to be hospitalised. He agrees you're in shock but he proposes to sedate you to calm you down, reduce the effect of the shock—you'll still be able to talk to the police, if you wish, but if you prefer not to we only have to tell them that you're under sedation and they'll go away.'

'Sedatives? That's what's in the hypodermic?'

He nodded.

She sighed. 'Oh, well, then, I suppose I'd better let him inject me.'

'I think you should. If the needle scares you, shut your eyes.'

'I'm not a child, Gil!' she snapped, and saw his lids flicker in reaction to her sharp tone.

He went out again and the doctor came back to the bed, prepared her; she tensed, waiting, and then she felt the sting of the needle going in and the doctor's soft murmur.

'Good, very good.' He put a piece of cotton wool over the site of the injection. 'Hold, please.' He moved away and Bianca sat with closed eyes, one finger on the cotton wool, feeling her body slow down, her breathing slacken, her heartbeat calm.

'OK,' said the doctor, taking away the cotton wool. He studied the faint red spot on her skin where the needle had entered. 'Good, OK,' he said, smiling, well pleased with himself. 'Now rest, please. Stay quiet. OK?'

'OK,' she said. 'Thank you, Doctor.'

'Goodnight,' he said in English, and vanished.

Gil stood in the doorway, staring at her across the room as she lay back against her pillows, staring back at him blankly.

'Will you see the police now or tomorrow?'

'Now.'

'Sure?'

'I want to get it over with. At the moment I feel so calm that if a bomb dropped I think I'd hardly blink. Tomorrow I might feel worse than I do now.'

'Do you want to put a nightdress on before you see them? They'll want that dress for evidence.'

She tried to sit up but her energy was so low it was a struggle; Gil slid an arm under her and lifted her, then lowered her feet to the floor. 'Tell me where to find your nightdress and I'll help you.'

'No!'

The cry made him jerk. 'No,' he said quickly. 'Of course not—sorry. I wasn't thinking. I'll find the nightie for you and go out while you change.'

'There's a clean one in that drawer,' she said, pointing, and he walked over there, opened the drawer, found a simple blue and white cotton Victorian-style nightdress.

'Will this do?'

'Yes, thank you.' She held out her hand and he gave her the nightdress. 'Now I'd like to go to the bathroom, please.' She stood up and swayed, and Gil put an arm out. 'No, I can manage!' she said, but felt sufficiently off balance to clutch at his sleeve.

She leaned on him while she slowly walked to the bathroom, which seemed a long way off.

'Don't lock the door,' Gil said. 'In case you faint.'

She didn't answer, but she didn't lock the door because she had to admit that fainting was definitely on the cards. The room was coming and going in a most disconcerting fashion, as though her vision was disturbed, but she knew it was her brain which was not operating at full strength. The injection must have been pretty strong stuff, whatever it was.

In the bathroom she pulled off the red dress, dropped it on the floor, in a tumbled heap, then turned on the shower and stood under it, washing herself from head to foot, feeling unclean. A few minutes later she towelled herself roughly and then slid into her nightdress.

Barefoot and damp-haired, she went back and found Gil in the last stages of making the bed with fresh linen. The used bedclothes lay in a pile on the floor, crumpled and untidy. She gave them a distasteful glance then looked away.

'Thank you, that was very thoughtful. Why didn't you call a maid to come and do it?' she said as he straightened to look round at her, his dark hair tumbling over his forehead, a lock half covering one eye.

'I thought you would rather not have anyone else around just now.'

His sensitivity touched her. 'No, I wouldn't,' she admitted huskily. 'You're very kind, Gil, taking all this trouble.'

'It's no trouble; you forget I was working in hotels when I was still a boy. It's my family trade. I can make a bed faster than the speed of light!' He grinned at her. 'There isn't a job in a hotel that I can't do efficiently. Anything I ask my staff to do I can do better!' He paused, then added more soberly, 'And also the police want your bedclothes, to take away for forensic examination.'

Shivering, she grimaced. 'Of course. Stupid of me not to think of that.'

She climbed back into bed and Gil tidied the covers with deft, practised hands. 'Can the police come in now to talk to you?' he asked her quietly. 'They're waiting in a car outside.'

She took a deep breath and nodded, and he brushed a few damp strands back from her bruised face, his fingertips cool and soothing on her hot skin.

'Do you want me to stay with you this time, to translate for you?'

She couldn't meet his eyes. 'Do they speak English?'

'A little, but not too well,' he told her regretfully. 'If you don't want me here, would you like me to find Freddie and get her here to help with the language barrier?'

She looked at him then, eyes stricken. 'She knows?'

Gil stared back at her, his face tight, his mouth a white line. 'I had to explain why you wouldn't be at dinner tonight. Don't look like that! Freddie isn't going to think any the worse of you because you've been attacked by that vicious little swine! You're hardly to blame for what happened! Why should you feel guilty?'

'Because I'm stupid and I'm a woman,' Bianca burst out, her voice shaky. 'Women have an in-built guilt pro-gramme—it starts when they're just little girls; whatever happens to them they are the ones who are made to feel guilty. It's always their fault. They're in the wrong place, at the wrong time, they're too attractive, they were wilfully wearing make-up, or pretty clothes—there are a hundred excuses for blaming them.'

'Freddie's a woman—she isn't going to blame you.' He paused and added roughly, 'And neither am I! It was bad luck that you ran into this nasty piece of work right at the start of your holiday. Maybe I shouldn't have insisted on calling the police, getting you involved in this investigation—you'd never have seen that little bastard again if I hadn't interfered.'

She lay back, calming again, and gave him a wry little smile. 'No, Gil, it isn't your fault either. You were right— I had to tell the police. Sooner or later he was bound to move on to more violent crimes than snatching handbags—he was going to use that knife, and I think he'd have killed someone, not merely raped them. He's dangerous; he had to be stopped.'

He nodded. 'I know. But I wish it hadn't been you who had to face that ordeal.'

'I'm tougher than I look. I can cope. I've had plenty of practice in coping with tough situations.' She thought of the long, hard birth of her first child; she had been very young then and very scared, but she had come through that, and through all the problems since; she had somehow even managed to survive Rob's death and the loneliness she had felt ever since. 'I'm pretty tough,' she added with a touch of self-congratulation, and Gil looked at her with sardonic amusement.

'You don't look so tough to me!' He ran a hand down her loose, silky black hair, lightly touched her bruised cheekbones with one fingertip. 'I wish to God I could have stopped this happening to you, Bianca.'

She inwardly flinched at the contact. If only he would stop touching her. In some ways he was so sensitive. Why couldn't he work out how she felt at this moment—as if she would never want another man within feet of her?

'Ready for the police now?' Gil moved away and she relaxed again, with a smothered sigh of relief.

He went out of the room; she heard him opening the front door of her apartment, then the sound of other voices, a heavy tread of feet, and the room seemed to fill up with policemen.

In fact there were only two and they were clearly trying to be quiet and sympathetic—but she found their presence so disturbing that she felt as if there were half a dozen of them.

Gil stayed throughout the interview, translating for her. Although she was very nervous, it turned out to be less of an ordeal than Bianca had been afraid it was going to be. The police were very down-to-earth and practical with their questions, and gradually Bianca relaxed.

While she was being interviewed one of the police team moved silently about the room taking fingerprints from door-handles and other places which the suspect might have touched, and another man wearing transparent plastic gloves gathered up the bedclothes from the floor and her torn dress and underclothes from the bathroom, stuffing them all into large plastic bags. As he carried them out Bianca watched him, her throat closing in revulsion.

Another man with a camera was waiting to take pictures of her face, showing the bruises which were rapidly darkening, the skin shiny and stretched around her eyes, on her jawline, around her mouth.

She jumped as the flashbulbs popped, and knew she was going to look like a scared rabbit, her eyes red and very big.

At last they went, and Gil got up too. 'You ought to eat—no, don't shake your head at me. You'll feel better if you have a light supper. How about an omelette? And some fruit? I'll have them send it over at once. What would you like to drink? A hot, milky drink would help you sleep. There will be a security man outside the block all night so if you need help you only have to yell out the window, remember.'

'I'll be OK. With that boy in police custody I shall feel a lot safer.'

He nodded. 'I'm sure you will. Goodnight, Bianca. I hope the rest of your holiday with us is going to be good deal less dramatic and far more pleasant.'

When he had gone she lay there staring at nothing. She couldn't stay on here; she had to get away. She had to go home. She would have to come back for the trial in due course, but that would not happen for a long time.

Her meal arrived quickly; the middle-aged waitress who brought it did not look at her face, keeping her eyes lowered as she murmured a greeting which told Bianca that Gil had warned the woman not to stare at her. No doubt the whole hotel was gossiping about what had happened—even the other guests would have noticed the arrival of police cars, the departure of the suspect, rough-handled into a car and driven away. Bianca hated the idea of being talked about by a lot of strangers.

'You eat in bed?' the waitress asked Bianca, hovering with her tray.

Nodding, Bianca sat up straight with pillows piled behind her, and the waitress carefully placed the tray in front of her.

'Anything else you want, please to ring,' said the waitress, without lifting her eyes, and left with the usual, 'Buen provecho!'

The herb omelette was excellent; Bianca ate most of it, with a little green salad, drank all her wine, then, feeling rather better, lay down and surprised herself by going to sleep almost as soon as her head hit the pillow.

She slept through the night, too, and woke up with a start when some people walked past outside talking loudly. Yawning enormously, Bianca didn't remember for a moment what had happened the night before, and then the memory came back with a thud like a blow and her eyes flew wide open. She sat up, looking hastily at the clock, and was stunned to see that it was around nine. She had slept for about eleven hours!

It was the best night's sleep she had had since she got here, and she was amazed by that until she thought it over and realised that knowing that that young thug was in custody and would not, this time, be released, had lifted a pressure from her mind. She had been subconsciously worrying about him ever since the first night here, when she was attacked in Marbella.

She slid out of bed and opened her shutters; another bright, sunlit day. She stared at the blue sky and felt positively unreal. Everything around her looked like the advertisement for a wonderful holiday, but for her it felt more like a nightmare.

She turned away and went into the bathroom to shower, then stopped dead in front of the mirror, staring at herself in shocked dismay.

The bruises on her face were all the colours of the rainbow this morning. She certainly couldn't face going over to the dining-room for breakfast; the idea of walking about getting curious stares was more than she could bear. She gingerly touched her face with a fingertip, wincing. How long would it take to get back to normal? Days?

She showered slowly, enjoying the clean feel of water on her face and body. The bruises were throbbing again, hot and stiff under her skin; she sighed with pleasure as the cool water ran over them. After a while, she towelled herself dry and wandered out to her bedroom to get dressed, but the phone rang as she was looking through her wardrobe.

'I saw you had opened your shutters so I knew you were awake at last. How are you this morning?' Gil's voice said softly.

She caught back a sigh, wishing he hadn't rung her. She didn't want to see him, talk to him; she wanted to forget they had ever met.

Carefully she said, 'Oh, hello. I'm fine.'

'Hmm,' he murmured. 'I'll come over later to see for myself.'

'No!' she broke out involuntarily, then hurriedly added, 'I really don't want to talk to anyone at the moment. I thought I'd just rest today.'

He sounded unsurprised and approving. 'Very wise; in fact, I'd stay in bed if I were you—the doctor thought a day or two in bed would be a good idea. I'll send Room Service over right away with some breakfast—what do you want? Anything cooked? Or just continental breakfast? Coffee or tea? Fruit juice?'

'Coffee, orange juice, rolls, cherry jam,' she said flatly. 'Thank you.'

'Get back in bed, then, and your breakfast will be with you in ten minutes.'

She looked at her bed as she hung up the phone, and decided to do as he said. Her energy levels were low this morning, she couldn't go out anyway—why not spend the morning in bed? She could always get up this afternoon. First, though, she made her bed, and when it was pristine put on a new pink lawn nightie, climbed back into bed and lay back against the pillows, staring at the blue sky outside, listening to the birds and the sound of the sea.

There was a tap on her door and then the sound of a pass key being used. She turned her head lazily to give a polite smile to whoever was bringing her breakfast, and stiffened as she met Gil's eyes.

'Room Service,' he said, advancing across the bedroom with a laden tray.

She should have guessed; why hadn't she? Or had she secretly been expecting him?

No! she told herself angrily. Of course not. I'd have got dressed if I'd even suspected he might turn up!

'Short of waiters this morning?' she asked him coldly and he grinned, those grey eyes teasing.

'I told you, I can do every job in the hotel trade; now, do you want to eat in bed or out on the balcony?'

'In bed,' she said, sitting up so that he could lay the tray across her knees.

Gil's eyes flicked over her nightdress; a delicate, pale pink, it had no sleeves, a low neckline and the soft folds of it clung to her full breasts.

She felt a surge of panic and ostentatiously inhaled the fragrance of the coffee. 'That smells good!'

'Hungry?'

'A little.' She poured herself coffee, sipped her orange juice.

He drew a chair near the bed and sat down. Was he planning to stay while she ate her breakfast? God, I hope not, she thought, spreading jam on a roll while she secretly watched him through her lowered lashes. I really can't cope, not this morning; I don't want to have him near me.

'Don't let me keep you from your work!' she said, and Gil gave her one of his amused looks, his mouth twisting in sardonic appreciation.

'My assistant is in charge, and you needn't worry— I'm not intending to stay. I just wanted to see for myself how you were...'

'Well, now you've seen!'

'Yes. You're as prickly as a cactus—which is good, I suppose. At least it's better than finding you weeping into your pillow. You're far too tough to collapse under pressure, though—aren't you?'

She gave him a cross look. 'You sound disappointed. Would you rather I was the weepy sort?'

He grimaced. 'Certainly not! Stay just the way you are.' He got up, leaned down and kissed her on top of her head. 'I'd better get back to work. Stay in bed; someone will come and collect the tray later. Anything you want? Magazines? Books?'

She shook her head. 'I have plenty to read, thanks, and I have my personal stereo and half a dozen tapes to play in it.'

'Well, if you do need anything, just ring the hotel.'

She watched him leave, feeling stupidly regretful and at the same time relieved. She needed to be alone; she felt like a snail which had lost its shell and needed to build itself another one.

The day went faster than she had imagined it would She dozed a good deal, read, listened to music—at one o'clock a waiter brought her a selection from the cold buffet table, chosen for her by Gil, she was told. Salad cold rice jewelled with tiny fragments of sweetcorn, peas red and green peppers, slices of cold, cooked chicken large pink prawns, and a thin slice of pink salmon. He had chosen an apple mousse for a pudding. It was so light it melted in the mouth and had a delicious flavour

Gil rang her that evening to ask what she wanted fo supper and she told him she wasn't hungry; she planne to eat a tin of soup she had, with toast, and some fresh fruit.

'I want to get to sleep early,' she added.

'Good idea; rest is what you need. The police rang couple of hours ago, by the way—they've charged him and he will not be given bail, so you don't need to worry about him any more. It will be months before the case comes up in court, too. They'll want you to make formal statement before you go home, but there's no hurry about that.'

She sighed. 'OK.'

'Goodnight, Bianca,' he said gently, and put the phone down.

Tears stung in her eyes. She felt unbearably sad, as i watching something die.

She couldn't bear to think about him any more—tha was the truth. She didn't want to see him, hear his voice be reminded of him in any way. Remembering how she had felt the first time she'd seen him made her wince she wanted to forget she had ever felt that way. It was too close to the horror of that moment in the apartmen when she'd seen the lust in that boy's eyes as he' stared at her.

Oh, the way she felt about Gil was nothing like that! That boy had wanted only to hurt, to humiliate. That was not how she had felt whenever she looked at Gil. She had felt pleasure in his male beauty, had yearned to touch him, to caress him—it wasn't the same at all. That boy had wanted to despoil, to degrade—the direct opposite of love, the other side of the coin, the dark side of desire. Nevertheless there was a subterranean connection in her mind. The two emotions seemed to her to come from the same source, from the instinctive reactions of the body. She was ashamed of having wanted Gil that way; it made her feel sick whenever that secret link was made. She kept shuddering, almost retching, at the memory, and each time alongside the memory of the boy's vicious, gloating eyes she thought of Gil and flinched.

She was glad to put out the light and get to sleep a couple of hours later, and she slept deeply again, in spite of having been in bed all day. She woke up early, showered, and got dressed in white cotton jeans and a blue T-shirt; the clothes were chosen instinctively and it was only when she saw herself in them, in the mirror, that she realised why she had picked them—they were such cool, neutral colours and made her look businesslike, less feminine.

It was odd, the way the mind worked, she thought, grimacing at her reflection. Her choice of clothes was a disguise, a protection. There was something almost childish about that that made her laugh even though she felt more like crying. With faintly shaky fingers she brushed her damp hair and tied it up in a ponytail—pulling her hair off her face, giving herself a severe, nun-like look.

A thin young Spaniard from Room Service arrive
with her breakfast a few moments later. On the tray wa
a note from Gil with a red rose in a thin glass vase. Sh
flushed as she glanced at the note, aware of the waite
watching her.

'Good morning!' was all Gil had written but the ros
was a wordless addition to the message which made he
very tense.

She had to get home. She could not stay here.

There appeared to be nobody about outside in th
gardens or the swimming-pool so she asked the waite
to carry the tray out on to the balcony, and when he ha
gone she ate breakfast in the early morning sunshine
safe from prying eyes, staring through the luxuriant
semi-tropical trees to the distant blue of the sea.

Gil's red rose had a delicate scent; she kept lookin
at it, her breath catching in a sigh of regret.

If only...

But there was no point in starting a sentence with thos
words—there never was any point in wishing things wer
different. You just had to face up to the reality of you
situation, and get on with life as you found it.

She had to forget about Gil.

How do you do that? her mind asked bitterly. The
had got to know each other so fast—the days they ha
been together had flashed past with lightning speed an
yet they had both learnt an incredible amount about eac
other. She had known others for a much longer time an
never found out as much about them.

Time had behaved in a very strange way since she'
arrived in Spain. She seemed to have been here forever—
yet it was just under a week since she'd started he
holiday. It gave her vertigo to contemplate the way tim
had whizzed past and then dragged; no wonder she wa

azed and confused! Looking back, she remembered grimly how she had come here for a rest. A peaceful holiday, relaxing in the sun, by the sea, was what she had been looking for.

Peaceful! These few days had been among the most eventful of her life! She was exhausted. She needed a holiday to get over her holiday. Except that she didn't want another holiday—she wanted to go home.

Yet she couldn't face the journey looking like this! People would stare; she could just imagine how they would sneak sideways glances at her, whisper, conjecture...it would be a nightmare.

A movement among the trees startled her. She looked down and saw Gil watching her. He raised a hand, walking towards the apartment block.

He was coming to see her. Her heart skipped a beat; she felt colour creeping under her skin.

She was expecting him to ring her front door bell, and decided to open it but not admit him. He did ring the bell, but he did not wait or give her time to decide what to do—having rung, he immediately used a pass key to admit himself and walked in, so that they confronted each other in the sitting-room a moment later.

He was not wearing his dark, hotel manager uniform today—instead he was wearing a smoothly tailored pale beige linen suit, a soft brown shirt, no tie, his collar open at the throat, showing her the beautiful golden skin that had made her notice him the first time she'd seen him.

He studied her closely, his eyes searching. 'Did you sleep? You look better this morning.'

'I'm fine.' If only he wouldn't stare! She felt his gaze on her skin as if he were touching the bruises, and flinched.

He noted the tiny movement and frowned. 'Does you
face hurt much?'

'It throbs a bit.' What sort of question was that
Stupid man, she thought. Of course it hurt; it was painf
every time she smiled or frowned.

'I'll get the hotel nurse over to put some more ointmer
on the bruises.'

'I can do it myself—if she could supply the ointmen
please.'

He nodded. 'OK, but I think she should see it th
morning, just to check on you.' He paused, looking a
her gravely. 'Have you decided whether or not you wa
to go home? The other night you said——'

'I know what I said!' she interrupted with impatienc
because he had touched on what was mostly botherin
her at the moment. 'I meant it—I do want to go home
but...' she gestured towards her face, her eyes angr
'...not while I look like this!'

'You'd frighten the life out of your children!' h
agreed, smiling at her, and her mouth curled into a r
luctant smile in reply.

'I was thinking more about getting stared at all th
way from here to England, but you're right—it woul
give Tom and Vicky a shock.'

'Do they know you were mugged?'

She shook her head. 'It didn't seem a good idea t
talk about it on the phone. It might worry them.'

'And it would worry them even more to hear wha
happened last night!'

'I'm sure it would.'

'Will you tell them when you get home?' He co
sidered her drily and she gave him a defiant look.

'I'll tell them I was mugged, I expect—I'll have to, t
explain why I need to come back here for the court case

'But not that you came close to being raped?'

She looked restlessly away, frowning. 'I couldn't,' she admitted. 'I doubt if I'll ever tell anyone that, except when I have to, in the court, but especially not my children.'

'You're very protective towards them, aren't you?'

'Well, I'm their mother, and they're both still very young and——'

'You're young yourself,' he said, looking into her blue eyes, a quizzical expression on his face.

Her flush deepened and she felt a little stir of irritation; she snapped at him, as if resenting him, which was ridiculous because her age was hardly his fault, 'I am not young—I'm forty!'

'Still obsessed with your last birthday?' he mocked, laughing. 'Bianca...don't you realise that your age has its advantages? A woman of forty is at her sexual peak—young girls don't know how to enjoy sex; for one thing they're still too inexperienced—they don't know enough about their own bodies to know what they're doing, let alone have a clue how to give a man the deepest pleasure. Love needs time, you know that; if you hurry it it's like gulping down food—you lose half the enjoyment. Young girls are usually in too much of a hurry; they don't have the patience or the confidence to take love slowly, make it last. Whereas a woman of your age——'

'Oh, stop it!' she muttered, flushing at the soft, husky tone of his voice because it was making her blood stir and her breathing quicken. 'I'm middle-aged and well aware of it. I have a nineteen-year-old daughter! When I'm out with her it's Vicky men stare at, not me, so don't give me any more stuff about men preferring older women!'

'Young men of Vicky's age, maybe! Perfectl[y] natural—young men usually feel much too insecure t[o] risk being turned down if they make a pass at an olde[r] woman. Try looking in the mirror, Bianca, instead o[f] gloomily telling yourself you're old. You're a very a[t]tractive woman; I'm prepared to bet you weren't as a[t]tractive when you were twenty as you are now. You'v[e] got style, you dress beautifully, you know what suits yo[u,] you don't try to follow fashion mindlessly—oh, f[or] heaven's sake, you know what I mean!' He moved im[-]patiently, his eyes challenging. 'Stop being so hung u[p] about your age!'

'You'll be forty one day yourself. See how you fe[el] then!' she threw back at him.

'I can tell you this—I won't go around telling myse[lf] I'm too old to get a woman!' he said, his grey ey[es] glinting with amusement and mockery.

She gave him a cross look. 'No, well, life's loaded [in] men's favour! They don't think they're too old to get [a] woman even when they're eighty!'

He laughed aloud. 'And why should they? Life [is] meant to be lived, after all. Now listen—you don't wa[nt] to stay shut up indoors all day, do you? That would [be] very boring, especially as it's going to be hot today. [I] suggest you come for a drive with me up into the mou[n]tains. There isn't much traffic on the roads up ther[e.] You could get some fresh air, see a new part of the regio[n] without having to endure people staring.'

She was tempted. He was right—it was boring bei[ng] shut indoors all day, and she felt restless, but she w[as] intensely nervous of being with Gil, afraid of the wa[y] he made her feel. It would make her sick if her bod[y] flared with desire at his touch; her stomach churned [at] the very idea of it.

'No, I can't,' she muttered, but gave a yearning glance at the blue sky outside.

'Don't be stupid, Bianca!' he said drily. 'What are you going to do all day? Just sit in here brooding? Get out into the fresh air, give yourself something else to think about. Come on, Bianca, I won't take no for an answer.'

That was what she was afraid of.

'You're going to have to, Gil,' she said, looking him in the eye and lifting her chin at the same time to make it clear that she was deadly serious.

She saw his eyes narrow and his face tighten. He had heard the undertone in her voice; he knew she meant more than a refusal to go for a drive with him today.

'I'm going to sunbathe on my balcony and rest for a few days—and then as soon as my bruises heal enough I'm flying home,' she added, walking away from him towards the front door. She opened it and held it open pointedly. 'Have a nice drive, Gil.'

He came towards her, his face shuttered, stopped and looked down at her. That was when she got a chance to see his eyes; they were smouldering, a smoky ash colour with a dark fire burning at their centre.

She felt a stab of pain, looking away from the threat of those eyes. Gil was angry with her. She was sorry about that. She hadn't wanted to make him angry; she liked him. Liked him far too much.

Oh, come on! she told herself. It's more than that and you know it. You fell for him like a collapsing wall the instant you set eyes on him. It was like seeing all your private fantasies come true—there he was, in the flesh, quite literally, tall and dark and golden-skinned, and you couldn't stop staring at him. It was plain and simple lust.

No! she thought, wincing. And, even if I did feel that way on sight, I liked the man too, when I got to know him. He's easy to like. He's amusing, good company, he's been unendingly kind and thoughtful and he's oddly sensitive for such a very macho man. I'm grateful to him and I wouldn't want to hurt his feelings.

But she had to protect herself—she could not face any more emotional pressure. She was like someone with severe burns who couldn't bear to be touched at all; the lightest fingertip could make them scream.

'I'm sorry, Gil,' she said. 'Please go.'

For a second, she thought he was going to argue, to grab her, to try coaxing or pleading, his whole body was so tense—but then he suddenly walked away without a word and she shut the door on him with a low moan, then leaned on it, her eyes closed, trembling violently.

It was over.

CHAPTER EIGHT

BIANCA'S bruises took days to heal, and she did not go out of her apartment at all during that time. She didn't go down to the beach and she didn't walk across to the hotel for meals—she either had Room Service or prepared meals herself in her little kitchenette. She was rapidly running out of the food she had bought just before the attack, but by the time the cupboard was bare she hoped her bruises would have faded enough for her to feel up to visiting the hotel shop again. During daylight hours she ate on her balcony with her back to the garden so that she couldn't be overlooked, and in the evening ate inside.

Every day she sunbathed on a lounger for part of the time, she read the books she had brought, she watched TV or listened to her personal stereo. The routine soon grew a little boring, she had so few distractions, and time began to drag, but it was also very peaceful and she was getting a lot of rest, which was, after all, why she was here. She had come to Spain for sunshine and rest—well, she was getting both.

It did surprise her that she didn't see anything of Gil as the days went by. She knew enough of him by now to know how tenacious and determined he could be; she had fully expected him to ignore what she'd said and turn up on her doorstep with every intention of talking her into going out for a drive with him. He didn't. He didn't show up in person—and he didn't ring her either.

In fact, she didn't hear from him at all. He might just as well have dropped off the edge of the world.

She told herself she was relieved. She told herself it was what she wanted. But she couldn't stop thinking about him, and she kept catching herself looking out for him in the garden below her balcony, her eyes searching the trees for a glimpse of him walking from the beach to the hotel, or back again. She knew he swam every day, either in a pool or in the sea. She expected him to pass her apartment building sooner or later, but if he did she must have missed him.

She did, however, have a visitor on the morning of the fourth day. When someone rang her doorbell she was out on the balcony, sunbathing, and she jumped up, startled, stubbing her toe on the leg of a chair.

'Ouch! Damn it!' she muttered, hobbling to the door, her breathing fast and her skin hot.

It would be Gil, of course. She would send him away again because she had meant what she'd said—it was over—but she couldn't stop the rapid beating of her heart or the quiver of eagerness to see him that she felt as she opened the door.

But it wasn't Gil standing on her doorstep. The eagerness died, her heart slowed back to a normal beat.

'Oh, Freddie! Hi!'

Freddie was wearing a pair of brief white shorts with a white T-shirt. She looked fabulous, much younger than her age. Her tan was even deeper, her eyes very bright, her short, blonde hair bleached to the colour of summer wheat.

She smiled at Bianca, her eyes flicking sympathetically over her. 'You poor girl—how are you? You're looking much better than I'd expected... those bruises are wearing off, aren't they? I'd have come sooner, but

Gil told us you didn't want visitors. I didn't like to be too pushy. We're going home in a couple of days, though, and I did want a chance to see you before we left.'

Bianca held the door open, smiling wryly. 'Come in and have a drink with me.'

They sat on the balcony in the sunshine, sipping ice-cold diet cola, talking lazily in the shade of an umbrella which fluttered in the faint sea breeze.

'Are Karl and the children on the beach?'

Freddie nodded. 'Where else? Gil is down there too.'

Bianca stared out across the gardens, the pulse in her throat beating with feeling. So he had gone down to the sea after all—and she had missed him. No doubt he had walked down there every day, but never at a time when she was looking into the gardens. She wondered if he had deliberately chosen a route that avoided her building, or a time when he might expect her not to see him.

After a little silence, Freddie said, 'What's wrong, Bianca? Between you and Gil? I know something is— he bites my head off whenever I mention you.'

Was he so angry with her that he hated her now? Anguish tore at her; she felt her throat burn with unshed tears.

'There's nothing wrong,' she said in a voice made husky by the salt in her throat. 'We saw each other a couple of times, but it was nothing important, and...and really I'm not the type for a holiday romance. I shall be going home myself shortly anyway.'

'Is that what you said to Gil?' probed Freddie, watching her with a sympathy that Bianca resented; she did not want Freddie being sorry for her or understanding how she felt.

'I would rather not talk about it, if you don't mind, Freddie!' she said stiffly. 'If Gil wants to tell you what we said to each other, that's up to him.'

'He wouldn't tell me a thing!' Freddie told her frankly.

'Neither will I.' But, contrarily, Bianca wished she knew what Gil was thinking, how he had really reacted to her decision. Freddie had said he bit her head off if she mentioned her—but what did his show of temper mean precisely?

Freddie shrugged. 'OK. You're both very irritating people, you know that?' But she smiled to show she was teasing, then gave Bianca a closer stare, hesitated, and said, 'You could disguise them, you know. The bruises, I mean—let me put some cover-up make-up on them. You'll be amazed when you see what a difference it makes. People will have to come up really close to see them and even then they'll be very faint, just shadows under the make-up.'

Bianca was tempted, but she shook her head. 'I'll look like a tart!'

'Don't be silly! I'll do it very...oh, what is the word? Er...discreetly—yes, that is it—discreetly. Please, I'm very good with make-up. I'm a member of our local amateur dramatics society. I help out with everyone's make-up during a show—even if I'm not in the play myself.'

'Do you act?' Bianca was interested; she had always wanted to join an amateur group herself, but she'd never had the time when her children were small, and by the time they were growing up Rob had died, and she had had to start work, leaving her no time for hobbies.

Freddie grinned at her. 'When they give me a part! I am not brilliant, but I enjoy it, and so does Karl sometimes—except he rarely has the time to take a part.

There's so much work involved—rehearsals, learning the words—a production takes over your life for weeks, and he is simply too busy. It's such a pity he can't act more often because he has real talent—far more than I do! I enjoy helping out with the backstage work as much as the acting, and I enjoy doing the hair and make-up— so, will you let me try some make-up on your bruises tomorrow morning? Then you can come down on the beach with us. You must be tired of sitting around on your balcony or inside your apartment, yes?'

Bianca hesitated, then took the plunge. 'OK, thanks, Freddie.'

It was quite true, after all. She was tired of staying around her apartment; she wanted to go down to the beach, swim in the sea, enjoy the last few days of her holiday here.

Next morning Freddie arrived after breakfast with a large make-up box and a determined glint in her eye.

She spent some time working on Bianca's face, gently smoothing foundation into her skin, to give an even layer, before she slowly painted out the bruises with a fine brush, finishing by adding a top layer of powder and blusher. When Bianca saw herself in the mirror she blinked. The make-up had been done brilliantly—oh, her lips were still faintly puffy, and there were cracks and cuts under the lipstick that Freddie had applied, but her facial bruises had almost gone; there was just a bluish shadow under the smooth, creamy make-up.

'That's amazing!' she breathed. 'Freddie, you're a genius! Even I can barely see a sign of a bruise. If I didn't know they were there I'm sure I would never notice them.'

Freddie looked modestly satisfied. '*Danke. Das freut mich.*'

'I'm sorry...I don't know any German, I'm afraid.'

'I said thank you...'

'Oh, I got that bit—but what did the rest mean?'

'*Das freut mich*? It means...I'm glad, or that makes me happy.'

'I must learn some German,' Bianca thought aloud.

'Yes, you must—I'll teach you some.' Freddie gave her an approving look. 'German is a very formal language and the grammar is complicated, but I'm sure you will soon pick up enough to be able to talk to people a little.'

When they got down to the beach Karl and the children were swimming in the sea. None of the other people down there gave Bianca a second look; they were all too busy sunbathing or playing beach games. She was able to settle down on her mattress under an umbrella, clamp her headphones on her ears and start reading a book. Freddie lay next to her, also reading.

Totally absorbed in her book, Bianca didn't hear anyone approaching until a pair of bare, tanned feet came into her line of vision. She looked at them idly, then slowly her gaze moved up the long, dark-haired legs, the lean hips in a smooth-fitting pair of black swimming-trunks, the flat midriff and muscled, golden-skinned chest to the familiar spare-fleshed features.

Her heart beat painfully.

'Oh...hello...'

Was that her voice? It sounded so shaky; she was furious with herself for betraying what was happening to her.

He gave her a grim look, frowning blackly, and if she had wondered how he had taken her dismissal a few days ago she knew at that instant. Gil had been furious; still was. She didn't know whether she had hurt his feelings or merely wounded his ego—whatever the case, Gil hadn't liked being told to take no for an answer, to go away and stay away.

His wife had damaged his ego years ago, leaving him for a much older man, but he had got over that. Maybe it had left him hypersensitive to any other rejections, though?

She should have thought of that. She could have thought of some gentler way of explaining why she wanted to end their brief relationship, couldn't she?

'So you've finally come out of hiding, have you?' he muttered. 'I was beginning to think you would stay in your rooms until you were due to fly home!'

That was what she had intended, of course, but she couldn't think of anything to say in answer to the accusation. But that didn't matter because he had hardly finished speaking when he did a visible double-take, starting physically as he took another long stare at her face. His expression abruptly changed, his grey eyes widening.

'Good heavens...your face... Your skin's back to normal... How on earth did those bruises heal so quickly?'

'Freddie worked a miracle,' she said huskily.

He blinked, looked even more closely, his black brows rising. 'Freddie did what?'

'Make-up,' Freddie informed him, sitting up on her mattress, her arms clasped around her bare knees. 'It's all done with make-up, darling.'

Gil shot her a sideways look. 'That's incredible—I can barely see any bruising at all; her skin doesn't show a thing. I wouldn't have believed it if I hadn't seen it with my own eyes. Freddie, my congratulations.'

She gave him a modest smile, teasingly fluttering her lashes. 'Thank you, Gil, dear. I thought it was time she stopped hiding in her apartment and joined the rest of us in the sun.'

He nodded, his gaze returning to Bianca, who had sat up too. 'I agree. At least you're looking better than you did last time I saw you; you were like a refugee from a Hammer horror movie! I hope you're feeling as good as you look?'

'Yes, thank you,' she said, not quite meeting his grey eyes.

'Sleeping well?'

'Yes, thank you.'

'Hmm...' he said in a dry tone. 'I suppose you've been eating in your apartment? You must have run through most of your food by now. If you need anything from the hotel shop, by the way, you know you can ring them and order it, and have it delivered?'

'Thank you, I'll remember that.'

They were talking like strangers on the surface, their voices polite and impersonal—but their eyes were at war. She kept her lids half closed, hiding herself, shutting him out, but she continually felt the probing of her defences, the quick, shrewd stare fastening on her quivering mouth, her restless hands, her nervous, half-veiled eyes, the vein beating in her neck, every tiny betraying signal of her body language. Gil wasn't buying her withdrawal, her cool manner towards him in front of Freddie. He was trying to find out what she was really thinking and feeling, and he was far too good at guessing.

That was the last thing Bianca wanted. She was struggling with her feelings, trying to suppress them; she didn' want him to have an idea what she was going through just having him so close.

'You've got sand on your arm,' he said, and leaned down, brushed his fingertips lightly over her skin.

Her heart winced with pain. The brief touch was enough to waken every pulse in her body and make her ache for him; her skin began to burn with instant reaction and she felt him watching her, reading her every slightest response with the efficiency of a Geiger counter.

I must get away from him, she thought desperately. I can't bear this. Shame made her stomach clench. She had hoped that these physical reactions were finished with, but they weren't, and that frightened her. She had always believed that desire was part of love, but to love you had to know someone completely, to know all about them—and what, after all, did she know about Gil? They had only met for the first time less than two weeks ago. Two weeks was a blink in the procession of time. She had known Rob for a long, long time before she'd got engaged to him.

But you never felt like this about Rob! she told herself, her heart sinking. When did Rob ever make you burn to touch him, to give yourself to him there and then——?

Stop it! she thought, shuddering. Stop thinking that way.

'Why don't we all have dinner tonight?' asked Freddie, and Bianca quickly answered, very flushed and agitated.

'I'm sorry, I really would rather have an early night tonight. I'm still trying to get plenty of rest.'

'Tomorrow night, then?' asked Freddie. 'We're leaving, remember. We won't get another chance to have that dinner party.' Her voice was coaxing, full of sunny warmth. 'Do say yes, Bianca.'

Bianca couldn't turn her down; it would have been rude and unfriendly and she didn't want to be either to Freddie. She took a reluctant breath, then nodded.

'OK, then, tomorrow night,' she promised, and Freddie beamed, then looked at her brother-in-law.

'What about you, Gil? You'll come, won't you?'

His grey eyes flicked to Bianca's face, reading the nervous expression in it without difficulty. His mouth twisted; she quickly looked down, and heard him say in a soft, deliberate voice, 'I'd love to, if Bianca is going to be there!'

Freddie laughed. 'I thought you would!'

Bianca bit down on her inner lip and winced at the bruising which still stiffened her mouth.

Gil went on, 'But I have to drive over to Nerja in the afternoon, to walk around the new hotel site with my architect. I'm not meeting him until four, and the meeting may take some time, so I may be late back—can we make dinner at half-past eight?'

'Is that all right with you, Bianca?' Freddie asked her, and Bianca shrugged, still avoiding Gil's gaze, her mind working frantically. So he was going to be out all afternoon tomorrow!

'Yes, fine,' she mumbled.

There was a yell from the edge of the sea and Freddie glanced that way, waved and got up.

'Karl wants me—be seeing you, Gil.' She ran off down the beach and Bianca felt her body tense immediately. This was what she did not want—to be left alone with Gil. She was terrified of what he might say or do next with his sister-in-law out of the way.

Hurriedly, to distract him from whatever he might have in mind, she asked, 'Did you say you were planning a new hotel somewhere?'

'Yes, at Nerja.' He was standing over her, his dark shadow somehow threatening, making her shiver.

'Where's Nerja? Near here?'

'Along the coast from Marbella, about an hour's drive. This is a very busy coastal road with a string of crowded resorts spaced out along it—it can take you an age to get from one town to the next; it all depends on the volume of traffic. If the roads are clear I might make it to Nerja in three-quarters of an hour; if there's a lot of traffic it could take me an hour and a half. Why?' His grey eyes narrowed on her. 'Would you like to come along for the ride?'

'No,' she broke out, the pulse in her throat beating furiously at the very idea of being alone with him again, even if only in a car.

A silence fell.

'Bianca——' he began, his voice harsh, and she had to stop him, could not let him finish that sentence.

In a stiffly polite voice she interrupted, 'Thank you for asking me, but I have taken to having a siesta in the afternoon.' Then she went on with barely a pause, 'Why are you building a new hotel? Are you bored with this one?'

'No, not at all, but I have got this place running very smoothly; it can almost run itself now, so I want the challenge of a new project.'

Was that the way he lived? Moving from one challenge to another? Hadn't Freddie said something along those lines? That Gil was restless, always moving on...was that the way he ran his private life too? Did he move on from woman to woman?

She hadn't thought he was that sort of man, but what did she know about him?

place is going to be a sports complex as well ,' he was saying with obvious excitement. This ubject close to his heart, she could see. 'The hotel w. .be surrounded by a competition-size golf course, I'm building a series of tennis courts, and an Olympic-sized swimming-pool—and I shall have a staff of top professionals in all the sports to coach visitors.'

'Won't all that cost a lot of money?' she said, taken aback.

'Millions,' he agreed cheerfully, and she looked up, eyes wide. He must be far richer than she had suspected!

He smiled wryly at her. 'I'm not risking all my own money—I have a partner—an American hotel chain which is keen to invest in this part of Spain. They are putting up a large chunk of the money, I am supervising the project here, and when the hotel complex is finished I'll be managing it for the first two years. Meanwhile, I'm training my assistant manager to take over here full time.'

'It sounds fascinating—and it's just the sort of hotel my son would love—Tom is very keen on sport of any kind.'

Gil's eyes were intent. 'He's the fifteen-year-old? Have you talked to your children lately? How are they coping?'

She relaxed now that they were on such safe ground. She was always happy to talk about her children. 'Fine, they claim, but I suspect they're living on take-aways and junk food. Goodness knows what the house looks like, too; I only hope they'll make some effort to tidy up before I get home.'

Gil gave her a quick, narrowed glance. 'You're here for another three days, though, aren't you? You booked for a fortnight, and you're on a special flight back; it can't be changed.'

She nodded, fighting to keep all expression out of her face, not wanting him to guess what was in her mind. Knowing that he was going to be out all afternoon tomorrow had given her an idea. She would ring the airport later and see if she could book herself on to a scheduled flight back to England, then she could pack her case, order a taxi and check out of the hotel without Gil knowing anything about it. She would leave a letter for Freddie apologising about dinner tomorrow night.

Freddie ran back, flushed and out of breath after a vigorous swim. 'It's wonderful in the sea today, Gil! The water is perfect; it's warming up nicely now, but it's so refreshing!' She threw herself down on her mattress and towelled herself, put a fresh application of suntan oil on her smoothly tanned skin, and lay down in the sun with a sigh.

Bianca lay down too, and picked up her book rather pointedly.

'Well, I'll go and have a swim myself, then,' Gil said, watching her. 'I'll see you both later.'

Bianca watched him run down to the sea, his tall, lean figure attracting a lot of attention—she saw other women lifting their heads to stare openly, their eyes skimming over that golden-skinned body in the brief black swimming-trunks.

'Gorgeous, isn't he?' Freddie said softly, and Bianca gave her a startled look, flushing.

'What? Oh...'

Freddie grinned at her, refusing to let her deny it. 'You know he is! And he's a very nice man, too; he's terrific company, but he's also thoughtful and kind-hearted. You can trust Gil, Bianca. If I weren't so fond of my husband, I'd jump at Gil myself.'

Bianca forced a laugh. 'I won't tell Karl you said so!'

'Oh, Karl knows how fond of Gil I am—and he's fond of him, too. He was my brother-in-law, but for years now I've thought of him more like a brother.'

Bianca was touched by the sincerity in her voice and sighed. 'That's nice, Freddie. I know he's fond of you too.'

Freddie gave her a hesitant, uncertain glance. 'My sister didn't make Gil happy; I know the failure of his marriage upset him for years. He is the sort of man who should be happily married; he has a lot to give any woman... I wouldn't want him to get hurt again.'

Bianca flinched and didn't know how to answer. A silence fell, and then Freddie put on her headphones and began listening to music, and Bianca could give her attention to her book, but she couldn't concentrate on it; the story and characters simply didn't hold her.

Freddie certainly knew Gil. Had known him for years. If she was so fond of him, he had to be as nice as he seemed. The thought did not make Bianca any happier. She didn't want to hurt him. But she couldn't trust the powerful instincts that worked in her every time she set eyes on him. It was a madness, this terrible desire; it wasn't love—it wasn't anything she had ever known before. She was afraid of it.

She kept sneaking a look down the beach, seeing Gil's sleek black head bobbing like a seal's in the sunlit blue sea. He was a vigorous swimmer; his brown arms cutting through the waves effortlessly.

She watched him as he came out of the sea, a glittering, wet, golden figure, the sun striking refractions from his skin so that he almost seemed to have an auriole, a radiance, surrounding him. He walked back up the beach, running a hand over his wet hair to rake it back from his face, picked up his white towelling robe from chair where he had left it, pulled it on with an elegant shrugging movement and tied the belt around his waist, slid his long, narrow feet into a pair of beach sandals.

A woman sat up to speak to him and he turned, smiling, his face in profile like the image of a Pharaoh in an Egyptian wall-painting, the black hair slicked to his head.

Bianca felt a stab of jealousy, and looked down to focus on her book, her breathing rapid. She had no right to care how he smiled at other women, she reminded herself; he did not belong to her.

'I'll see you tomorrow,' he said suddenly right above her, and she started, not having heard him coming.

'Oh...did you have a good swim?'

'Wonderful—you should try it! Don't just lie in the sun all afternoon—get into the sea!'

'Maybe I will,' she agreed, her eyes briefly meeting his.

It was a mistake. She felt her mind dissolving in waves of sensual reaction and hurriedly looked away.

At what seemed a far distance she heard his voice a moment later, saying curtly, 'See you at dinner tonight, Freddie.'

She heard him moving away and couldn't look; she was still fighting to get over the swimming feeling in her head. Instead, she stared fixedly at her book and pretended to be reading.

She had to get away from him. She couldn't bear much more of this. If anything, it was getting worse. Just seeing him made her body clamour terrifyingly.

She planned frantically... She would go tomorrow, while he was in Nerja. She would make all the arrangements about her flight and a taxi over the phone in the morning, pack, eat a light snack in her apartment at lunchtime, and wait until she was sure Gil had left before she went over to the hotel to pay her bill and wait for the taxi.

Once she got back home and picked up her life where she had left off she would soon forget all about this holiday, and about Gil.

Of course, she would have to come to testify in the court case when it was finally heard, but that probably would not come up for months. For the moment she could forget about that.

She could forget about Gil, too.

It sounded so easy, so simple and reasonable. Why then did she find herself gripping the edge of her book so tightly that her knuckles had turned white? And why couldn't she see the printed words on the page, except through a blur of tears?

She rang home that evening and told Vicky and Tom that she was coming home early.

As she expected, they were not wild with enthusiasm. 'Tomorrow? Why...? When tomorrow? We'll have to tidy up; why didn't you let us know earlier?' moaned Vicky.

'I only just decided,' said Bianca. 'You hadn't got party planned or anything?'

'No,' Vicky said, sounding warily devious.

'Had one already? House still in a mess?' asked Bianca.

Vicky was sulky. 'What is this—an interrogation Well, if I've got to tidy this whole house up tonight I' better start right away, and Tom is doing his share of the work too. Most of the mess is his anyway.'

Bianca put the phone down, smiling to herself. She could imagine the panic in the house this evening. The

would be screaming accusations at each other as they
rushed about. She was glad she wasn't there.

She didn't sleep that night, and was up early next day;
she began to pack immediately after breakfast. She rang
the airport and was able to book herself on to a flight
at five-thirty. She rang a local taxi firm and ordered her
taxi for two o'clock. Gil should have left by then, but
would give her plenty of time to drive to the airport
and check in.

She was intensely nervous, afraid all the time of Gil
appearing and discovering her plans, but everything went
like clockwork. She checked out of the hotel, got her
taxi and promptly at five-thirty took off in the plane,
landing at Heathrow as scheduled.

She got home after dark and found Vicky and Tom
waiting for her and the house looking immaculate,
smelling of lavender furniture polish and daffodils. Every
room downstairs had a vase of daffodils in it, their yellow
trumpets lifting the heart.

'Everything looks wonderful,' she said generously,
giving her two children a hug.

They looked smugly pleased with themselves. How
long had they had to work to restore the house to
normal? she wondered, but didn't ask. Instead, she
produced the presents she had bought for them during
her time in Marbella. Vicky was delighted with her hand-
painted fan and her silk-fringed Spanish shawl, and Tom
seemed very happy with his shirt and hand-made leather
belt.

'Gosh, you're brown, Mum,' he said, staring at her.
'Mum ... are those bruises on your face?'

She put a nervous hand to them, as if to cover them
up. She was wearing heavy make-up, but even that

couldn't hide the bruises entirely, although they were
fading now.

'I'll tell you about them over supper,' she said.

Vicky had made a quiche; a vegetarian version full of
broccoli, onion and tomato cooked in cheese, it was
served with a green salad and small new potatoes and
was quite delicious.

'Wonderful cooking, Vicky,' Bianca congratulated her

'Well, don't think I'm doing all the cooking in future!
she retorted tartly. 'This was a special occasion. I can
tell you, I'm glad you're back to take over; I'm sick of
tidying up after *him*.' She glared at Tom who glared back

'I wasn't the one who had a party that went on all
night!'

'You haven't got any friends to invite to a party!
snapped Vicky, and Tom made gargoyle faces at her.

'Don't squabble,' Bianca said, then smiled at them
'I really missed you both; I'm glad to be home.'

Vicky gave her a surprisingly adult look, frowning
'Did you really have a good time, Mum? Why did you
come home early? You still haven't told us how you got
those bruises.'

Bianca took a deep breath, and gave them a carefully
planned explanation of the mugging, playing down the
violence and the fear she had felt. Something of it must
have come through, though—they both looked shocked

'How ghastly! Thank heavens you weren't badly hurt
and nothing worse happened,' said Vicky. 'No wonder
you're back home early!'

'I wish I'd been there,' Tom muttered, his face flushed
and his neck rigid with belligerence. 'I'd have taught the
little swine a lesson! You shouldn't have gone on your
own, Mum. Next time I'll come with you.'

Touched, she smiled at him.

In bed that night, she lay awake in the dark for an
our, fighting memories of Gil, and wondering how long
t would take her to forget about him.

Judy was amazed to see her back when she went into
he shop next day. 'Bianca! Good heavens! I wasn't ex-
ecting you until next Monday! Love the tan—it suits
ou—you should always be that colour!' She grinned.
You must have had good weather! Why are you back
arly? Didn't the holiday romance work out after all?'

'I got mugged,' Bianca told her, to distract her from
uestions about Gil.

Judy exclaimed much as Vicky and Tom had done,
er eyes widening in disbelief. 'No! You're kidding!
Vhat happened!'

Bianca gave her the same mild version of events that
he had given her children, leaving out all references to
he second attack, and Judy bombarded her with ques-
ions, peered closely at the bruises on her face, asked if
he was going back to be a witness, asked how she had
elt when it happened, said that she would be happy to
ccompany Bianca when she had to return for the court
ase.

Bianca couldn't admit why she certainly would not
ant either her children or Judy to go with her. She was
eginning to be afraid that when the case did come up
e English newspapers might pick up on the story of
e attempted rape. If they didn't, she might never need
tell anyone here what had really happened. She was
reading having to give evidence in a Spanish court,
nyway. She wished now she had come home after the
rst attack; the second one would never have happened
en.

She asked Judy, 'How did you get on on your own in
e shop? Any problems?'

'None at all, I managed perfectly,' Judy said with
touch of high dudgeon, tossing her head. 'We were ver
busy on Friday and Saturday, as usual, and I was ru
off my feet then, but the rest of the week things wen
like clockwork. No problems.'

'Well, now I've had a break, why don't you have one
Judy?' Bianca suggested.

'It doesn't sound to me as if you had much of
holiday,' Judy said drily, and Bianca couldn't deny tha

'I was unlucky, but there's no reason why you shoul
be!'

'Well, I'll think about it,' Judy said, and then a cu:
tomer came in and, with a smile, she went over to de:
with her while Bianca went into their little office to mak
coffee for them both.

It was all so normal and familiar. She felt as if sh
had never been away. It would be easy, here, to forge
about Gil, she told herself, ignoring the wince of anguis
she felt at the thought of him. All she had to do w:
face each day as it came and keep all thought of him :
bay. He would fade in her mind the way the bruises o
her face were fading.

It might have worked out that way—if she had ne
come home from work the following Monday evenin
to find an Alfa-Romeo parked outside her house. He
heart turned over violently. It was Gil's car.

CHAPTER NINE

BIANCA stopped to stare at the car, saw it was empty and looked anxiously around for Gil; there was no sign of him. Suddenly she realised that he must be in her house—which meant...

Oh, no! she thought, beginning to run. Someone must have let him in, which meant he was in there now, with one of her children, talking to them! And what would he be saying? She didn't want to guess. Whatever he said, his mere presence here would arouse Tom and Vicky's curiosity and she would find herself being pestered for answers once he had gone.

A wave of warm fragrance from a bed of hyacinth beside the house hit her; they had only come out today, deep purply blue and white, her favourite colours in the garden, but, although she unconsciously registered their scent, she didn't even stop to look at them—any more than she stopped to look up at the budding cherry tree on the lawn which came into blossom every spring. Most evenings when she came home she paused to take in every changing aspect of her garden. It was all part of her familiar home life, the patterns of the year, of which Gil was no part. His arrival was like a stone thrown into a calm pond; ripples were widening in all directions and she could think of nothing else.

As she fumbled for her front-door key in her handbag her fingers trembled; at last she found it, put it in the lock and hurriedly opened the door. As she stepped inside she heard Gil's voice and smothered a groan. He was talking to Tom. They were laughing, Tom's the deep, hoarse laughter of a teenage boy whose voice only broke a year ago and who hadn't yet attained his real adult voice.

Bianca shed her black and white hound's-tooth check jacket, took a quick, nervous glance at the mirror in the hall, wished she were wearing something more glamorous than an old blue sweater and back skirt. She smoothed a few strands back into her chignon, checked on her russet lipstick, took a deep breath, and went into the sitting-room.

Tom and Gil were standing in front of a row of family photographs on a table by the window. Laughing.

Bianca glared at their backs, opened her mouth to say something barbed—then Gil turned to look at her and she felt her body turn weak and tremble.

'Hello,' he said, and smiled, and her heart turned over and over like a tumbler turning somersaults.

She thought she wasn't going to be able to say anything at first, and then she got out a husky, 'Hello,' and Tom turned round too.

Bianca couldn't quite meet her son's eyes. 'Have you offered Mr Marquez a drink, Tom? Would you like some coffee, or something stronger? I think we may have some sherry somewhere.'

'Coffee would be fine, thank you,' Gil said, and his eyes had not moved from her for a second; she hoped Tom hadn't noticed the way he was staring.

She flickered a look at Tom, and he was staring at her too, looking a bit pink; she knew he was upset because his ears were pink as well, and that was a sure sign with him. She had not shown a serious interest in a man since his father died and Tom was at that sensitive, half-boy half-man stage where anything out of place or unex-

pected could embarrass; he was obviously taken aback
to have a strange man arriving out of the blue to see his
mother.

Tom still had a simple attitude to her. She was *his*
mother! Why would she want another man, a life of her
own? She had him, didn't she?

'Would you make the coffee, please, Tom, while I talk
to Mr Marquez?' she asked him, hoping he wouldn't be
difficult. She had to get him out of the room. She
couldn't talk frankly to Gil with her son there, listening
to them.

Why had Gil come? She hadn't thought he would do
this; it had not entered her head that he would follow
her. She had assumed he would just accept the fact that
she had gone, and put her out of his mind.

'Right,' Tom said in his gruff, not quite grown-up
voice, and stumbled out, making a lot of noise as he
slammed the door behind him.

He's angry with me! she thought, sighing, and then
realised that the room was very still, yet reverberating
with awareness. Her nerves prickled. She hurriedly
looked at Gil and saw his eyes flash, the smile vanish
from his face as if wiped off with an invisible hand. That
was when she realised that Tom was not the only one
who was angry with her. Gil was even angrier—his body
was as taut as stretched wire, and his eyes glittered.

'Did you really think I'd let you end it like that,
without so much as a word?'

He took a step closer, and she felt her stomach sink
as if she were in a lift which had suddenly gone out of
control. Gil angry was frightening; he made the room
seem suddenly very small. He looked oddly out of place
here, in England; his tanned skin, black hair and light

eyes made him look distinctly foreign under these cool grey English spring skies.

She fought to hide her nervousness; with men and dogs you had to pretend you were unconcerned and in control, especially when you weren't. They were quick to pick up any uncertainty in you.

Lifting her chin, she defied him. 'I wish you hadn't come here,' she said, and he laughed with bared teeth, taking another stride.

'I bet you do! That's why you ran away, isn't it? You couldn't actually face the thought of talking to me, admitting anything . . .'

'There's nothing to admit!' she threw back, bristling like a frightened cat.

'Liar,' he said, moving closer again, and his grey eyes were violent—they seemed almost black. 'You were scared so you ran away—don't tell me there's nothing to admit. I should have guessed you would try something like that, of course. I knew you were tied up in knots in your head.'

'My head is none of your business!' He had guessed how she felt, and that frightened her even more. She didn't want him knowing what she was thinking or feeling. She needed the privacy of her own head; she didn't want him invading it. It meant he knew too much about her.

'Everything about you is my business,' Gil said softly. 'I'm in love with you.'

The blood seemed to drain out of her heart. She went white, then red, breathing fiercely.

She had never realised before how close to pain some joy could be; her body couldn't sustain such anguish, she was afraid she would die of it, and yet she had never felt so alive.

'I fell in love with you the minute I saw you on that balcony, staring down at me,' she heard him say. The words seemed to come from a long way off; she gazed at him, fighting for breath. Gil reached out and framed her face in his hands, his palms warm against her skin. He looked passionately into her eyes and her own eyes darkened until she could scarcely see him.

She couldn't fight it any more; she wanted him too much; just feeling his hands touching her sent her into a fever. She shut her eyes to shut out the world, reality, the fear which had been dominating her ever since that night in Spain. For one moment...just one moment...she had to give in to the way Gil made her feel. So she closed her eyes and sank into the darkness.

'Oh, Bianca,' Gil whispered, sending a shiver of desire down her spine. She was so afraid she was going to faint that she grabbed at his shirt to keep herself upright.

Touching him was a mistake. It was like lighting the fuse of a bomb; she felt the explosion right through her body, and so did Gil. She heard his intake of air, then his mouth hit hers.

Bianca shuddered, her palms flattening on his body, feeling the beating of his heart reverberating under her hands. She arched backwards, with his arm around her, kissing him back, her mouth parted, hungry. Her hands ran up his body and round his neck, closed on his nape, holding him. For the first time in days she felt real again, complete; Gil had somehow become necessary to her; without him she felt like someone who had had a limb amputated and was haunted by the absence of an essential part of herself.

But I'm forty! she thought with a pang of grief. I'm forty, and Gil's only in his thirties. When he marries again he'll want children, obviously; he hasn't got any—

of course he'll want some. And at forty the chances of
my having another child aren't very good. Possible, I
suppose—women of forty do have babies—but it isn't
as easy a process at that age as it is when you're in your
twenties; problems are more likely to crop up. It's far
more tiring to be pregnant; you and the baby are more
at risk. Oh, and even if I could have one quite safely,
she thought, do I want to go through all that again? I've
been along that road once, with Rob; I was the right age
to do that then; it was all new and exciting, being a wife,
having babies, bringing them up. But now Vicky is
grown-up and Tom certainly isn't a child any more. Do
I really want to start again?

And what on earth would they think of their mother
marrying again, having a baby? It's simply ridiculous;
it is out of the question. I had a wonderful marriage and
a marvellous man—it's greedy to ask for a second chance
at love.

Her mouth was growing cold and stiff under his; she
felt the excitement draining out of her. Gil broke off the
kiss suddenly and caught her chin in one hand, tilting
her head.

'Open your eyes, Bianca. Look at me.'

Her lashes fluttered against her hot cheek. She shook
her head.

Gil shook her slightly, his voice impatient, insistent.
'Stop being such a coward—look at me! I want to see
your eyes.'

Reluctantly she lifted her lids; her blue eyes were
shadowed and dilated. Gil looked into them, his face
just inches away.

'I know what's going on in your head, and it's crazy.
You love me, I know you love me—you couldn't kiss

me like that if you didn't—but you're so afraid to admit it that you'd rather ruin both our lives.'

'We barely know each other!' she whispered, tears behind her eyes. 'Can't you see how ridiculous it would be? We only met a fortnight ago! How on earth could I ruin your life by turning you down? This is just an infatuation, Gil, can't you see that? Go back to Spain— you'll soon forget you ever met me.'

His face darkened. 'Will you forget me?' he bit out, and she winced, trying to lie.

'Of course I w...'

The words died in her throat; she could not utter them.

Gil nodded grimly. 'You know you won't. And I'm not going to forget I met you either, not if I live a hundred years.'

'We'll both be dead in a hundred years!' She shrugged, forcing a laugh.

'Don't make light of what I feel, Bianca,' he muttered. 'I'm not going to let you do that. I made a mistake about my first wife—or maybe we were mistaken about each other. But this time it's different. This time I'm absolutely sure it's the real thing, Bianca—aren't you?'

His grey eyes stared insistently into hers. She stared back, swallowing, dry-mouthed.

'I may only have known you for a short time, but I'm certain you're the woman for me, Bianca, and I even think I know why you're trying to drive me away.' He paused, then in a gentle voice added, 'I understand, you know.'

A pulse beat at the side of her throat. 'What are you talking about now?'

'I understand what's wrong,' Gil said calmly. 'What scared you off was that little swine attacking you in your apartment, wasn't it? You got everything muddled up in your mind; suddenly you just wanted to get away from me. You were afraid of yourself and me—we'd moved too fast, maybe. But that was inevitable from the minute we met. I know I'd have jumped into bed with you the first day.'

She drew a shaky breath, her face burning.

Gil's eyes challenged her. 'Come on, admit it. I'm pretty sure you felt the same way.'

'I'm not admitting anything!' she mumbled.

He sighed. 'If only you hadn't gone into Marbella that first evening, been mugged—I've an idea everything would have been different if there had been no complications. But you confused what you felt for me with what that little thug tried to do to you. And that wrecked everything. I knew what was happening. I saw it in your face that night in your apartment when we caught him— I saw the way you couldn't bear me to touch you. Why do you think I left you alone when you told me to go? Do you think I wanted to go? Don't you think I was worried sick about you? I could tell what was going on in your head; it wasn't difficult to work out. I realised I had to leave you alone to get over the shock of being attacked like that.'

'Don't keep talking about it!' she broke out, shaking, icy cold as she remembered that night.

'Talking about it is the only way you'll get it sorted out in your head,' he told her. 'You should be having counselling, Bianca. You need to talk this out—a shock like that goes on echoing inside you for years if you don't deal with the trauma. If you deal with it, it will fade, the way the bruises on your face have faded.'

He put a tender finger on her cheek, trailed it down to her mouth, followed the parted, sighing line of it.

'Don't,' she whispered.

'I love you—don't send me away again,' he said. 'I've taken a fortnight off from the hotel, left my assistant in charge—give me a chance to get to know you better. Take some more time off; we'll explore Kent and London, go to the theatre, take walks, talk, find out all about each other.'

'I'm forty!' she reminded him desperately, afraid that he was going to give in.

He laughed. 'So you keep telling me. And I keep saying...so what? I'll be forty myself before long.'

'You'll want to have children and I don't think I want to go through all that again.'

'If I wanted to marry someone just to have children I could have done it any time these past few years. I'm not obsessed with having a child; if you don't want to have any, that's fine by me. I'm not even asking you to marry me, Bianca. I'm only saying I want to get to know you better.'

She met his eyes. 'You want to sleep with me—isn't that what you're saying?'

'You know I do,' he said huskily. 'I won't lie about that—I want you, I've said so, but not until you're ready.'

'And if I never am?'

He grimaced. 'I'll have to live with that, won't I?'

'Yes,' she said, her gaze defiant.

'All I ask is to see you every day while I'm here in England,' he said softly, watching her mouth with a hunger that made her tremble.

She heard Tom coming and moved away from Gil in a hurry, sat down on the deeply upholstered couch just as the door opened and Tom walked in, concentrating on carrying a heavy tray which held cups and saucers, a coffee-pot, cream jug, sugar bowl, even a plate of biscuits.

He avoided looking at them, and laid the tray down on the coffee-table in front of the long couch.

'Shall I pour it?'

'No, I'll do it,' Bianca said, picking up the coffee-pot. 'You only brought two cups, Tom.'

'I don't want any.'

He hovered, watching her fill a cup, add sugar but no cream to the strong black coffee which she offered Gil who took it and sat down next to her.

'This smells good,' Gil said, and as he spoke there was the sound of a key turning in the front-door lock.

'There's Vicky,' Tom said. 'What about supper, Mum? I'll start getting it ready if you tell me what we're having.'

'I was thinking of——' she began, but Gil cut in.

'Why don't you choose for yourself tonight, Tom? I expect there's lots of food in the fridge. I am taking your mother out to dinner.'

'I can't——' began Bianca, but he interrupted.

'Of course you can!'

'I have to make supper for Tom and Vicky.'

'Tom and Vicky are quite old enough to make supper for themselves,' he said coolly, and smiled at Tom. 'Aren't you?'

Tom did not smile back; he glowered.

Unconcerned, Gil said to Bianca, 'After all, they managed perfectly well while you were in Spain; why shouldn't they do so tonight?'

Before she could answer him, Vicky came into the room and stopped dead, staring at Gil, her hazel eyes rounding into saucers.

'You must be Vicky,' Gil said, holding out his hand and smiling in a way that made her look even more startled. 'Hello. I've heard a lot about you from your

other—I'm Gil Marquez; your mother and I met in
arbella while she was staying there.'

Vicky shook hands, stammered something, then
oked at Bianca as if her mother had suddenly grown
o heads. She was only too obviously putting two and
o together, and not far out with her guesswork.

'I'm taking your mother out for dinner tonight; you
o can manage without her for the evening, can't you?'
il said with a cool authority which brought a murmur
agreement from her two children.

'Yes, of course,' said Vicky.

'Mmm...' Tom said a little sulkily, shrugging.

Bianca couldn't argue with him in front of them. She
t up from the couch. 'I'll go and change, then.'

'Don't be long or I'll come and look for you,' Gil said
ithout caring what her children thought.

She gave him a furious look and hurried out. Upstairs
e chose a dress he hadn't seen, and was about to slip
to it when there was a tap on her door.

'Yes?' she called warily.

'It's me,' said Vicky.

'Oh...' Bianca sighed. She had hoped to avoid a dis-
ssion with her daughter until she got back later to-
ght, but obviously Vicky had no intention of waiting.
ome in,' she added.

Vicky came in, closing the door behind her. She looked
ldly younger suddenly, a little helpless, her mouth
intly prim, her hazel eyes accusing, as if her mother
d behaved badly.

'Who is he? You didn't tell us you'd got involved with
me Spaniard, and I bet I know why you kept him so
iet. Do you know anything about him? I mean, he
obably thinks you're a rich widow; he looks like a guy
 the make to me!'

'Vicky!' Bianca laughed with impatience. 'Yo
couldn't be more wrong! He has far more money tha
me and——'

'Oh, you're so naïve,' Vicky said crossly. 'These me
haunt holiday resorts just to pick up women like you.
mean, just look at him... all that tanned skin, that soli
gold Cartier watch, and those clothes—you should kno
they're high fashion. His suit's Armani, Mum! It wi
have cost an arm and a leg. And he's too good-lookin
to be real; he has to be a phoney.'

'He can afford Armani—he owned the hotel I wa
staying at!' Bianca told her, and Vicky's mouth droppe
open.

'You're kidding!'

'No, and it was one of the best luxury hotels i
Marbella—there were about six swimming-pools in th
garden complex, and it had its own private beach.'

'And... he owns it?' Vicky still wasn't convinced.

'Not only that, he's building another one, down th
coast, a luxury sports centre-cum-hotel. So forget an
idea of him chasing me for your father's insurance mone
or my shop. I'm not in the same league.' Bianca looke
at her watch. 'Now, I want to get changed—out you g
Vicky.'

Vicky was staring at her fixedly, mouth open. 'Wh
on earth does he see in you, then?'

'Go, Vicky,' Bianca said, furious and laughing at th
same time, and took her by the shoulders and pushe
her out of the room, locking the door behind her.

She took ten minutes to get ready and then stood
front of the dressing-table mirror in an agony of unce
tainty, staring at her reflection.

Vicky was right, after all. What on earth did Gil s
in her? What could he want with a forty-year-old moth

f two who wasn't sophisticated or witty or beautiful or ich?

Her blue eyes were as dark as the evening sky as she hought about it without coming up with any answer.

What did she want from Gil, come to that?

It was a mystery. She took a deep breath and turned way from the mirror. She wanted him, that was all she new. Maybe that was all Gil knew too?

She went slowly down the stairs and he stood at the ottom of them, watching her come, with an expression at made her shake with fever. Desire had its own asons that the mind could not explain.

From the sitting-room her two children watched her nd Gil, their faces baffled, disapproving, worried. Vicky nd Tom loved her and were afraid she might get hurt, e thought, understanding. She was afraid of that too, ut sometimes you had to take a leap into the dark.

'I'm ready,' she said huskily, and took the hand Gil eld out to her. They went out into the spring evening ogether. Bianca felt her heart lift at the scent of hya-nths and the soft fall of the dusk. Life was mysterious d unpredictable . . .

Coming Next Month

HARLEQUIN PRESENTS®

THE BEST HAS JUST GOTTEN BETTER!

#1845 RELATIVE SINS Anne Mather
Alex mustn't know Sara's secret. But her small son Ben adores
him and she has to admit that Alex is ideal father material....
Is the answer to keep it in the family?

#1846 ANGRY DESIRE Charlotte Lamb
(SINS)
Gabriella realized she couldn't marry Stephen and ran out on
him on their wedding day. But Stephen wouldn't take "I don't"
for an answer....

#1847 RECKLESS CONDUCT Susan Napier
(9 to 5)
Marcus Fox didn't approve of Harriet. She put it down to her
new bubbly blond image. Then Marcus reminded her of the
events at the last office party....

#1848 THEIR WEDDING DAY Emma Darcy
(This Time, Forever)
Once he was her boss, and her lover.... And now Keir is back in
Rowena's life. Can they let go of their past and forge a future
together?

#1849 A KISS TO REMEMBER Miranda Lee
(Affairs to Remember)
It was time for Angie to stop comparing every man she met with
Lance Sterling and move on. Here she was, twenty-four and a
virgin...and suddenly Lance was back in her life!

#1850 FORSAKING ALL OTHERS Susanne McCarthy
When Leo Ratcliffe proposed to Maddie, was he promising the
true love of which she'd always dreamed—or merely offering
a marriage for his convenience?

Harlequin brings you the best books, by the best authors!

ANNE MATHER

"...her own special brand of enchantment."
—*Affaire de Coeur*

Watch for:
#1845 RELATIVE SINS
by Anne Mather

Sara has a secret that her brother-in-law, Alex, must never know. But her small son, Ben, adores him. Sara has to admit that Alex is ideal father material, but his motives are a mystery to her. Is he playing a game to which only he knows the rules?

Harlequin Presents—the best has just gotten better! Available in November wherever Harlequin books are sold.

Look us up on-line at: http://www.romance.net

HARLEQUIN PRESENTS®

HARLEQUIN PRESENTS®

Dear Reader,

re: RECKLESS CONDUCT by Susan Napier
   Harlequin Presents #1847

Harriet had decided to change her whole image,
but Marcus Fox, chairman of the company she
worked for, didn't approve....

Yours faithfully,

The Editor

P.S. Harlequin Presents—the best has just
   gotten better! Available in November
   wherever Harlequin books are sold.

P.P.S. Look us up on-line at: http://www.romance.net

HARLEQUIN PRESENTS®

by Charlotte Lamb

A compelling seven-part series

Coming next month:

The Sin of Anger

in

#1846 ANGRY DESIRE

As she stared at her wedding dress, Gabriella realized
she couldn't go through with her wedding to Stephen.
The only way out was to run...but would Stephen
come looking for her...?

Love can conquer the deadliest of

Harlequin Presents—the best has just gotten better!
Available in November wherever
Harlequin books are sold.